WITCHBOTCHED IN WESTERHAM

Paranormal Investigation Bureau Book 9

DIONNE LISTER

Copyright © 2019 by Dionne Lister

ISBN 978-0-6487042-6-3

Paperback edition

Cover art by Robert Baird

Content Editing by Hot Tree Editing

Line edits by Chryse Wymer

Proofreading Hot Tree Editing

All rights reserved.

No part of this book may be reproduced in any form or by any electronic or mechanical means, including information storage and retrieval systems, without written permission from the author, except for the use of brief quotations in a book review or school assignment.

This is a work of fiction. Names, characters, businesses, places, events and incidents are either the products of the author's imagination or used in a fictitious manner. Any resemblance to actual persons, living or dead, or actual events is purely coincidental.

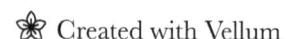

❈ Created with Vellum

Dedication

To Mum for always being there and encouraging me. xx

CHAPTER 1

The howling morning wind shrieked gleefully as it tore past me and Will as we made our way along the dirt path. I would've shivered in the near-zero temperature had we not just walked two miles. It wasn't exactly the best time of year to be visiting the White Cliffs of Dover—unless you loved the cold—but with all the craziness of PIB work, and Millicent ready to give birth any day, we weren't going to pass on a few hours to sightsee when the opportunity materialised. This place had been on my things-to-visit list, and Will was helping me tick them off one by one. Okay, so this was only about number three I'd covered since I'd gotten to the UK eight months ago, but it was better than nothing.

Will took my hand and led me closer to the cliff edge but stopped a respectable distance away, which could be measured in metres or a scale of "If Lily tripped and fell, how far would she fly and not go over the edge." I was estimating it was about eight metres. Even then, I was careful not to move too much, except to remove my camera's lens cap with gloved fingers and put it in my pocket. It may seem like overkill, but I'd hurt myself in way more innocuous circumstances, and with Regula Pythonissam after me, I'd come to expect the unexpected—Dana or one of her cronies could show up at any moment and push me over the edge, and then overkill would be less about exaggeration and more about me dying. Not cool.

I disentangled my fingers from Will's, turned the camera on, and raised it to my face. "It's absolutely gorgeous." The gale snatched my words and scattered them into the fields beyond, but Will must have heard because he replied.

"It definitely is."

I smiled when only the water, gradating from crystal-blue to dark, white-capped turquoise, showed through the lens. Seeing the past—including dead bodies—was an all-too-frequent event that still had the power to ruin my day. Having special witch talents wasn't all it was cracked up to be.

After clicking off some shots, Will and I kept walking towards the South Foreland Lighthouse and the quaint little café—Mrs Knott's Tea Room. Another woman passed us, heading the way we'd come from, all rugged up with a scarf wrapped around her face so only her eyes were showing. I gave her a wave and smile, but she ignored me. Hmm, okay. Talk about unfriendly. I shook my head—nope, I wasn't going to let a bit of unfriendliness ruin my day.

Will squeezed my hand. "You know the South Foreland Lighthouse was the first one to use an electric light?"

Good old Will, distracting me before I could get cranky about being snubbed. After all, the woman was just a stranger I would never know. Maybe she'd just had a fight with her husband, or maybe her best friend had just died, and she wasn't in the mood to communicate with anyone. I squeezed his hand back. "I didn't know that. What other titbits of information do you have to impart?"

"Well—" A chilling scream cut him off. We stopped and spun towards the cliff. Another couple stood there staring at the cliff edge. Will dropped my hand and ran to them. I was a bit slower—it wasn't like there were snakes or anything around here. What could the emergency have been?

"Is everyone all right?" Will asked the couple. They looked to be fortyish and fit. I could imagine them doing rock climbing or marathons.

The man had put his arm around his partner, her face paler than you'd expect someone's to be in the middle of an English winter. She kept staring at that one spot at the edge of the cliff. The man answered, his voice a pleasant Irish brogue. "We were walkin' along, and this woman comes from over there." He pointed back the way we'd come. "She just walks all determined-like to the edge and then just keeps on going."

The woman nodded, then shook her head, as if to say, wasn't that just crazy and horrifying. I tended to agree. Will looked at me, then back at the man. "Did she have a red scarf covering her mouth and nose?"

"Aye, that she did." Oh no. So, she had been having a terrible day. And me saying hello hadn't helped—not that it had made anything worse, but if only I could have stopped her and made her talk to me. Maybe I could've said something to make her feel better or stop her jumping. Oh God, she was likely lying smashed on the rocks at the bottom of the cliff or maybe floating face down in the water. I put my hand on my stomach to settle its protests and observed the other woman, who still looked whiter than white. No wonder. How horrible to watch someone do that... just give up and walk into oblivion.

Will pulled his phone out. "I'll call emergency services." We all nodded, no one saying a word. The wind buffeted us with an extra-forceful blast, as if acknowledging the horrible circumstances. How many people did jump off here every year? We had a place in Sydney called The Gap. It was a cliff on our gorgeous harbour, in one of our most exclusive suburbs, but the beauty of the place wasn't enough to convince people not to jump. My shoulders sagged under the weight of sadness. I wondered who the woman had been, and why she had jumped.

Will hung up and put the phone in his pocket. "They're on their way. Now we all wait."

And that ended our relaxing stroll for today. It was as if trouble found me wherever I went. Hmm, it wasn't *as if* it did—it actually did. At least this was a straightforward suicide. Argh, that sounded so insensitive, but you know what I meant. I wouldn't be asked to take photos or chase a criminal down. We could, hopefully, leave this behind when we went home, although it was depressing that my memories of Dover would be forever linked with this woman… this event.

As we waited, I stared out to the English Channel and spared a thought for the woman's relatives. Later today, their whole world would be forever changed, a little darker. I knew how that felt, and I wouldn't wish it on anyone, well, except maybe Dana Piranha. Thoughts of the horrible snake queen—yes, you totally could be a piranha and snake at the same time—led me to thoughts of my parents. We weren't any closer to finding out what had happened to them, with all the crimes we'd had to work on lately. And now that Millicent was about to have the baby, we'd been keeping to ourselves, trying to lay low, especially after the snake group had tried to kidnap her with a catch spell on her house.

Eventually the police and rescue team showed up. We answered their questions, and Will took one of the policeman's cards. Then we were free to go. By the time we walked back to the car at the visitor's centre, then drove the hour and a quarter home, it was twelve thirty. Will, being the dear he was, stopped at Costa for me to pick us up some lunch, which we took home to enjoy—being Saturday, Costa was full.

We walked into Angelica's house to high-pitched buzzing, then Olivia saying, "Oh my God, no!" Laughter followed, so it couldn't be too bad, whatever *it* was.

I called out, "Hello. We're back."

The buzzing stopped, and Liv said, "We're in the living room."

I shrugged off my coat and hung it on the hook in the small foyer. Will laughed, his coat popping into existence next to mine. "That's not very witchy of you, Lily."

"I like to remember where I came from."

He smirked. "More likely you forgot what you were. You really should get into witchier habits."

"Yeah, yeah, I know. It'll happen one day." Not automatically using my magic was okay in day-to-day life, but when I was consulting with the PIB, it was dangerous. Forgetting to put up a return-to-sender spell could be lethal. I really had to increase my effort, plus, using magic for lots of little things would make my magic stronger.

The buzzing started again. I wasn't sure what I'd expected—possibly a giant mosquito—but it wasn't this. Beren stood to one side of the living room, a small controller in his hand. Liv stood still, back ramrod straight, on the other side of the room, near the crackling fire. A red leather-bound hardback book sat precariously on her head.

Flying across the room towards Liv was a miniature helicopter. It zipped crookedly, then hovered before shooting forward again. The tip of Beren's tongue stuck out of his mouth as he concentrated. Liv said, "Argh! Careful." The helicopter almost hit her face. I clenched my jaw in anticipation of a bloody collision, but Liv was braver than me and didn't move. She scrunched her eyes shut, and the toy darted straight up, hovered, then slipped forward and slowly lowered to the book.

"I did it!" Beren grinned. The helicopter blades stopped spinning, and the mosquito noise stopped.

"Nice work!" Will held up his hand, and they high-fived. *Boys*.

I looked at Liv, who was still too thin after her horrible ordeal with Owen the Oracle's spell—which was more like a curse—had left her on her deathbed with a metabolism faster than a cat's lap of the house after it had done its business in the cat litter. At least she was back to eating normally, and on Monday, she was going back to work for the first time since she'd been arrested for something she wasn't responsible for. Kent Police had given her a written apology, and she'd been paid for the time she'd been off, plus they gave her extra time for stress leave—and so they bloody well should have.

Liv slid the book off her head and handed the toy to Beren. She looked at me. "What can I say? We were bored."

"Is that the thing my brother gave you for Christmas?" We'd had an awesome Christmas lunch at his place and then gone to Liv's parents afterwards. They still didn't know we were witches, which was lucky considering all the problems we'd had after Liv had gotten sick from that spell. So many people had to be mindwiped, and it took Angelica days to write the reports to present to the PIB directors. I still didn't know who any of them were, as it was the toppiest of top-secret information, or should that be secretest? Neither one was a word, but it needed something for emphasis.

Beren grinned. "It sure is. Best present ever." Olivia folded her arms and frowned. "Ah, second-best present...."

Liv raised a brow. "That's more like it."

Will slapped Beren on the back. "Don't worry. You'll learn."

"And who knows?" I smirked. "You'll probably beat Will to figuring it out."

Beren laughed. "Ooh, burned, brother." It was his turn to slap Will on the back.

My stomach grumbled. I looked down and patted it. "Okay, I hear you." I looked back up, and everyone was watching me, bemused expressions in place. I grinned. "What? Don't act like you've never seen me have a conversation with my stomach before. So, if you'll excuse me, I'm going to sit in front of the fire and enjoy my coffee and double-chocolate muffin."

"I'll join you." Will sat on the other armchair in front of the fire.

"Where's ours?" asked Liv.

"Sorry," I said around a mouthful of divine chocolate goodness. "I didn't know you'd both be here. Do you want some of mine?" I held out the muffin. I was loath to lose some, but she did need to get more calories into her, and I'd do anything for my friends, even go without my favourite food.

Liv smiled. "Nah, I was just joshing you. Beren, best boyfriend ever, actually came over early and cooked us a scrummy omelette and french toast."

"Oh my God, yum!" I turned to Will. "You really need to up your game. He's so far in front, it's not funny."

He rolled his eyes. "So, saving your life doesn't rate?"

I put on my best blasé tone and waved one hand dismissively. "That was ages ago. Besides, I returned the favour. What else you got?" I bit the inside of my cheek to keep from smiling.

He gave me his best Crankypants glare but spoiled it when the corner of his lips twitched. Giving up, he smiled. How could I resist those dimples? I grinned. "Well played, Lily. Well played."

"Why, thank you."

Will's phone rang. Our smiles disappeared. We gave each other a knowing look. His phone ringing was rarely a good thing and usually involved work. He answered it. "Morning, Ma'am." He listened for a while. "Okay, yes. See you soon." He put the phone back in his pocket. "Sorry, but I have to go into work."

I sighed. "At least we got to spend the morning together." Not that it had been all rainbows and kittens. That poor woman….

He swallowed his last mouthful of coffee and stood, holding his arms out. "Come here."

I placed my muffin on the table next to my chair and stood, then wrapped my arms around him. I tilted my face up to his, and we kissed. Mmm, I'd never get sick of his soft lips.

Beren cleared his throat. "Ahem. Get a room."

Will broke the kiss and lifted his head to look at Beren

over my shoulder. "Oh, I forgot to tell you—Ma'am wants you to come in too." His grin was all dimples and triumph.

"Seriously? It was supposed to be my day off."

"Say your goodbyes, Best Boyfriend Ever, and let's skedaddle." Will smirked. He gave me one last kiss. "See you later, gorgeous."

"Bye." I waved sadly as he stepped through his doorway. After Beren bade Liv goodbye, I sat back down, and she joined me.

"So, now what?" Her gaze travelled to the window and the clouds that had only just come in. We were supposed to get rain today, and it looked like it wasn't far away. It didn't make for wanting to do anything that involved going outside.

I would have suggested the gym, but she needed to eat more, not burn more, and the movies were out after last time turned into a trip to Hades. Hmm... I made a bubble of silence. "Hey, how about we go through my mum's diaries and pick something to investigate? It's the only way we're going to move forward, and with everything that's been going on and then Christmas, I haven't done anything about it." I was probably avoiding it a bit too because seeing them through the camera, so real yet untouchable, killed me. But I'd never find out what had happened to them or get the snake group off my back until I delved deeper. Not to mention that James and his baby were in danger until we shut Regula Pythonissam down.

"That works." Liv smiled.

"Great. I'll be back soon." I drained my coffee cup and

magicked it to the bin and the other half of my muffin into the fridge. Then I stood and made a doorway to the PIB. I'd get Ma'am to magic the diaries from the spell-protected vault she kept them in. I didn't even know where it was. Super top secret for all our benefits. At this stage, they were our strongest lead, although the snake group had no idea that I could see past events with my talent, and they probably had no inkling that my mother's diaries contained clues to her past with Regula Pythonissam.

The security guard who answered the reception-room door at the PIB was a new recruit—I'd met him a week ago. He was about thirty years old and ginormous—at least six foot seven from my estimation and built like a brick outhouse. His neck tattoo and shaved head made him look like someone you wanted to avoid and definitely not upset, but he was actually soft-spoken and super nice. Unfortunately, Gus hadn't returned from stress leave. He blamed himself for his boss's death, and nothing we said could convince him otherwise. We were considering an intervention because Gus was definitely not to blame, and we all missed having him around, despite his ability to turn any conversation to secretions.

"Hey, Clyde. How's things?"

"Just fine, Miss Bianchi. And how are you?"

"Pretty good, thanks. I'm here to see Ma'am. Is she around?"

"I'll check." He punched a few things into his tablet, then looked across at me—yes, my eye level was just about where he was holding the tablet. I felt like a child standing next to him. "Yes. She has a meeting in ten minutes, though, so you'd best hurry. She's in her office. Would you like an escort?"

"No thanks. I'm good. Have a great day." I smiled.

"You too." He returned the smile, pivoted, and walked the other way down the hall.

I quickly made my way to Ma'am's office. When I knocked, she called me through. "So, to what do I owe this visit?" She looked at me over her reading glasses from her chair.

I made a bubble of silence. "I wanted to grab Mum's diaries. Liv and I have time to go through them and figure out where I should go next."

"Right, well, before you decide anything, clear it with me. Also, you'll need to take Imani with you. She's not available today, but I can free her up for tomorrow."

I tried, I really did, but the eye-roll happened nonetheless. "Of course I know to take Imani. Sheesh. I'm not stupid, and I don't have a death wish."

She raised a brow. "You don't always do the sensible thing, dear. I feel I need to remind you at every opportunity."

I huffed and decided I'd never win an argument with her. I'd just pretend the last part of the conversation never happened. "Would it be possible to get those diaries today?"

"Yes, dear. Wait here. I'll be back soon." She stood and made a doorway but before leaving said, "Good choice, dear. You would have only dug yourself in deeper." She smirked, and then she was gone.

Gah. Thanks for rubbing it in. Angelica never missed a chance to be superior or bossy, but I knew she was doing it because she cared. Didn't make the sting hurt any less, though. At least no one else had been here to see my latest dressing-down. It was important to look at the positive side, wasn't it?

She soon returned, her arms filled with the five small books. "Here you are." She plopped them carefully on her desk, and a Waitrose Knives-and-Forks reusable shopping bag appeared next to them. I stood and put them in the bag. "Thanks. What time will you be home tonight?"

"I'm thinking around six. I'll chat to you about this then."

"Okay, thanks. I'll see you later." As she sat, I made my doorway and returned home. Now it was time to find out where to next. My stomach muscles clenched. Wherever it was, it wasn't going to be easy. But I had no choice. I had a mystery to solve, and the longer I left it, the more danger we'd all be in.

Not for the first time, I wished I were a squirrel. If only the most pressing thing I had to find were some nuts. I sighed and opened Angelica's reception-room door. "Liv," I called out. "I'm back. Let's do this." At least my voice sounded way more sure about this than I felt. As the saying went: fake it till you make it. I was becoming quite the expert. Now I just had to hope faking it wouldn't get me killed.

CHAPTER 2

It was just after midnight. One at a time, Will, Imani, and I stepped through our doorways into the out-of-order cubicle in the ICC Birmingham—a massive international conference centre northwest of London. Mum had been here a few months before Dana's mother had died. It seemed like an easy-ish target for me to investigate compared to the other one I was interested in: a ball at a French chateau, which was still owned by the same company and lived in. Angelica was running background checks on the owners.

Will had magically disabled the security cameras and alarms. We had a warrant from the PIB in case we came across a witch security guard. If we encountered a human one, Will was going to put them to sleep and mindwipe. Not ideal, but we had to do whatever it took to keep this secret—you never knew who was involved with the snake group, and the less they discovered about what we were doing, the better.

The event my mum had attended here looked innocent enough from what we could find in her diary and online—a fundraiser for a conservative political party. Because it was such a boring thing, I figured something must have been fishy about it. My mother wasn't into politics, at least not that I knew. Angelica had confirmed my assumption. While we were here gathering photographic evidence, my brother was researching the politicians who'd organised the event.

Will poked his head out of the main bathroom door first. He moved through to the hallway and waved for us to follow. Within a few feet, we came out at a main thoroughfare. Blue carpeted stairs with steel handrails overlooking the main concourse were to one side. I looked left and right, making sure no one was about to surprise us. It was dead quiet, the blue carpet muffling our steps as we made our way to the railing overlooking the ground-floor concourse of the centre five flights down. The glass roof was supported by a blue-painted steel Meccano set. Massive banners hung from the beams, advertising the ICC and a pet-food company.

I looked around again, then whispered, "Where to now?" I knew we'd come out on Level 5, which was where hall 8 was, but which direction to go now was beyond me.

"Hang on." Imani took a map of the centre out of her pocket and unfolded it. She had a quick look. "This way." She led us down the corridor and across a narrow walkway, which was really a bridge connecting one side of the upper levels with the other. I couldn't help but look down as we crossed. Oh, crap. Someone was down there, at ground level, walking along the centre of the place. A security guard. I moved faster, pushing Imani along. When we got to the other side, she turned and opened her mouth. I shook my head violently and pointed down. Her eyes opened in acknowledgement. I nodded and breathed out relief.

She turned and moved to the door that had a sign near it with a big blue 8. Imani led the way inside the dark room. I turned on my camera. Once Will was inside and the door shut, I asked quietly, "Do we dare turn on the lights? I can't see anything."

Will moved to stand next to me. He nestled a warm hand under my hair to rest on the back of my neck. Mmm, that was nice, except we weren't exactly in the right place to start anything. Still, we were in a dark room, standing close—could anyone really blame me for my thoughts going there? "You don't need light for what happens through your camera. Whatever is in the past will show up as it was that day, won't it?"

"Oh, yeah. You're right. My stupid." I put the lens cap in my pocket and pointed the camera towards what I assumed was the whole room. Since we were standing in the doorway, it stood to reason. "Show me my mother." I wasn't going to bother being more specific because I wouldn't think she'd been in this room too many times.

The room appeared to spring to life. Oh, a video moment! I quickly flicked the camera to video and pressed record. Unfortunately, I couldn't hear anything. The room was awash with red lighting. Banners hung on either side of the stage, proclaiming, "Only the powerful must lead!" and "Return the UK to Glory." A mass of round tables, each seating roughly ten people, crowded the room. A small stage with a lectern sat against one wall. A man was standing up there, addressing the crowd of well-dressed adults. His mouth was moving, but, of course, I had no idea what he was saying. I walked towards him, hoping I wasn't about to crash into anything in real time. I put one hand down to feel for chairs or other impediments.

I whispered, "I'm just walking to the far wall to get a better shot of something." I didn't want Imani and Will wondering where I was or whispering to me when I was too far away to hear.

"Roger that," Will said.

I haltingly progressed until I stood right in front of the grey-haired, dark-suit-wearing man. At this distance, we might be able to lip-read later. It took another minute, but then he finished speaking, smiled, and walked down the stairs off the stage… straight through me. I jumped back. Bloody hell. I put a hand on my chest and got my breathing under control, then panned the camera around the tables, looking for Mum.

I held my breath for a moment. There she was, in a red halterneck dress, her hair falling loosely around her shoulders. She was so beautiful. I blinked, banishing tears. Dana's father sat next to her, some bald guy on her other side. Where was my dad? I guessed they mustn't have done everything together, but all the other shots I'd taken in the last few months were of both of them.

Dana's dad leaned towards my mother, saying something that she was laughing at. Dana's mother—on the other side of her father—was smiling too, but it was more of a gritting of teeth and didn't reach her eyes. No way. Why would she be jealous of my mother? There was no way my mum would have an affair.

As I kept recording, Dana's mum patted her husband on the arm. He ignored her for a moment before he turned to her, smiling. She said something to him with a fake smile still plastered on. He nodded, his smile genuine—the poor sod couldn't see he was in trouble. As his wife left, he rested his arm on the back of my mother's chair. She didn't even flinch, either not noticing, which I couldn't believe, or not minding. What the hell was going on? Again I wondered where my father was.

Another man approached their table. Expensive charcoal suit, slicked-back ebony hair, he smiled with all the warmth of a shark. Dana's dad looked up at him, then stood. They shook hands. The new guy said something, and Dana's dad nodded. He appeared to excuse himself from the table, and they left.

The video stopped, my mother frozen in time, watching them go.

I flicked it back to camera. "Show me my mother." The image hadn't changed. I pulled my phone out and risked using the torch so I could find my way back to Imani and

Will. I left it on for a couple of seconds, got my bearings, and went to them. "Okay, that's it. I got some video."

"Video?!" Imani sounded excited. "Great work."

"Well, it's not like I can choose. You'll have to thank Lady Luck for that one. There was something else. You've put up a bubble of silence, Will?"

"Yes."

"Cool. Dana's dad was sitting at a table with my mother. But then he left with some slick-haired guy. I'm wondering if I should try and get some shots outside, just in case we can find him."

"But what would that tell us, Lily?" Imani had a fair question.

"I have no idea, but maybe body language can help us figure it out, or maybe if it's video, we can lip-read later?"

Will answered, "Okay, I'll give you a couple of minutes to figure it out, but we don't want to risk discovery, and they could have had their conversation anywhere in this building—we're not spending all night looking for them."

"Okay. Lead the way out, boss."

"You do know you don't respect that title as much as you should, right?" The smile in his voice shone through the darkness.

"I know, but that's one reason you love me."

Imani snorted.

The door latch clicked. "I wouldn't go that far, Lily." Will opened the door, and faint light seeped through. He checked no one was coming and led the way out. Once in the public area, I whispered, "Show me Dana's dad meeting with Slick." My magic knew who I meant, so I didn't need to know his name.

Nothing. Damn.

I lowered my camera, turned it off, and shook my head. "I guess it's time to leave."

Will nodded. "We'll all go to Ma'am's. She'll be asleep, but I want to watch that tape before we finish up."

I yawned. The mention of sleep must have reminded my body that it was way past my bedtime. "Sounds like a plan."

"After you," said Will. I made my doorway home, Imani and Will close behind. I wasn't sure what we were going to learn about my mother's time in hall 8, but I wasn't ready to concede she might have been having an affair. My mum, the woman who would hold my dad's hand when we were out, the women who looked at him with such adoration—that was the real her, wasn't it? And if it wasn't, what then?

For the first time, I really didn't know, nor did I want to. But there was no backing out now. I just had to believe there was a reasonable explanation for what appeared to be flirting. Besides, she wouldn't have put it in her diary if she didn't want me to find out about it, although she couldn't know I had a talent for seeing the past. Maybe the clues were meant to be in who had attended, rather than my mother's relationships with any of them. Or maybe it was just what the event stood for?

Whatever the reason, I was reserving judgement. Yep, no judgements being made... yet. But if that were true, why did the sinkhole in my gut feel like it was getting larger by the second?

CHAPTER 3

There's nothing as awesome as waking up with your cheek in a wet patch on your pillow… said no one ever. Argh. Even worse, Will was already out of bed and likely at work. What was the time? I sighed in resignation—it was time to get out of my dribble and face the day. Also, note to self: change your pillowcase before going to bed tonight.

I slid out of bed and clumsily grabbed my phone off my small desk. Ten thirty. A huge yawn almost dislocated my jaw. I eyed my bed wistfully. *No, Lily, you're not going back to bed.* My inner voice won—I didn't want to waste the whole day. I had things to do, one of which was to go to my brother's and hang out with Millicent. She was so close to her due date, and whenever someone had spare time, we were spending it there, just in case. After the scare with the catch spell a few weeks ago, we thought it was better if she wasn't alone. While I was there, I had photo editing to do. I'd covered a wedding on New Year's Eve. Such a crazy time to get married. I was their third choice of photographer—it seemed I was the only idiot willing to work on such a momentous day, but for me, it was like any other, and no offence to Westerham, or even London, but nothing matched the fireworks on Sydney Harbour we had every year. Plus, I wasn't a fan of standing outside in zero degrees waiting for said fireworks. Oh, and I was even less of a fan of reminiscing. With my past, it was likely to end in tears.

After washing my face, brushing my teeth, etcetera, I magically dressed myself, grabbed my bag and laptop, and travelled to Millicent's. She answered the reception-room door with a tired smile. "Lily! How are you?" She gave me an awkward, baby-bump-in-the-way hug. Her two dogs jumped up, greeting me. Normally, she had them locked away when I came over, just in case Liv was with me, but today, she knew Liv was working. "Down, puppies." They both settled, which I appreciated. They were medium-sized dogs and, if they put their minds to it, could probably knock me over.

"I'm great, thanks. You're looking gorgeous but tired. Is everything going okay?"

She shut the door and locked it. "Come in, and we can chat over a cup of tea." I cleared my throat, and she laughed. "Or a coffee." The dogs stayed protectively at her side as we moved through to the kitchen.

I giggled. "That's better. So, spill."

"It's just really hard to sleep with this." She rubbed her

belly as we entered the kitchen. "I'm sick of lying on my side. I can't even lie on my back because when the baby gets to this stage, it can put pressure on the umbilical cord, so it's dangerous. And when I do manage to sleep, baby dearest decides to kick and wake me up. I have a night owl on board." She walked over to the small table on the other side of the kitchen. "Let's sit here—it's more comfortable." The dogs lay on their beds in the corner.

I sat at the table and looked out the glass-panelled door into the frosty garden beyond. The familiar tingle of Millicent's magic gently feathered my scalp, and two cups appeared on the table. I savoured the rich coffee scent before taking a sip. "Mmm, nice."

"I got those Lavazza beans you keep raving about. James says thank you, by the way."

I grinned. Us Aussies loved a smooth brew, and we knew our coffee. It was a culture all its own in Australia—there was practically a café on every corner, and a good number of the population owned their own cappuccino machine. "Tell him he can thank me with some kind of awesome present for my birthday."

She laughed. "After that amazing photograph you gave us, I think he'd give you anything you asked."

I'd gone back to where he'd proposed and used my talent to take a photo of him proposing to Millicent. It still brought a tear to my eye when I thought about it. "It was the least I could do. He sacrificed so much to look after me after Mum and Dad disappeared. And you've been nothing but welcoming since I arrived. You guys are the best, and you're going to be the parents of my favourite niece or nephew."

She gave me a sly smile. "It helps that you don't have any others."

"But if I did, yours and James's kids would totally be my favourites."

She conjured a bubble of silence. "So, tell me what happened last night. James mentioned you were out at a diary entry."

"Yep, although I'm not quite sure what we've discovered. They might be great leads, or they might not. James is going through all the people in the video, finding out who they are. When he's got all that info, he'll call a meeting. I think he's reluctant to set dates for stuff because you guys don't really know when Baby Awesome is coming." I smiled at her bump.

She rolled her eyes. "Yes, well, I want it to be sooner rather than later. This body isn't big enough for the both of us." She laughed. "Seriously, I can't believe how much your skin can stretch, or how squished your organs can be and still work."

I nodded. I wasn't in any hurry to grow a human. It was way down on my to-do list. "It doesn't look like much fun, to be honest. But soon enough, you'll be back to your normal, trim self, able to tie your own shoelaces."

"Argh, you're not wrong. It will be a day I celebrate. I am rather puffy at the moment." She slid a foot out of her slipper. "See."

Her foot was twice its normal size, and her toes were like

frankfurters. Too late, I caught myself pulling an "ew" face. I hated feet at the best of times, and this was far from the best of times for Millicent.

Millicent sighed. "I know. It's gross."

"Sorry. I didn't mean to let that face out."

She giggled. "It's fine. I pull that face when I see my feet too. So, enough about my horrible, swollen feet, and more about other stuff. How's Liv going?"

"Really well. She's slowly putting on weight, and she's almost back to the energy levels of old. Beren's been the best through all of this. He's such a sweetie."

"He is such a great guy." Millicent winced.

"What's wrong?" I leaned forward, trying to see what was wrong, but there was nothing obvious. Had Regula Pythonissam managed to breach the spells protecting the house?

"It's okay. I just have a headache coming on." She rubbed her temples with the thumb and middle finger of one hand. "Probably just not enough sleep."

"You don't think it's the snake people?"

"No. They can't possibly get through all our protective wards. Don't worry." She shut her eyes.

"Should you lie down? Can you take anything?" I knew pregnant women couldn't just have any medicine they wanted. I had no idea what was okay, though. "Do you want me to call James?"

"I can take paracetamol." She squinted at me. "Can you grab me two? They're in the top cupboard, just there." She turned and pointed to the kitchen cabinet closest to us above the benchtop. I grabbed a glass, filled it with water, and popped two tablets out of the packet. She took them from me with slow hands. When she was done, I took the glass from her. Her complexion paled, and the tightness around her eyes revealed how much pain she was in.

"You don't look too well. Please go lie down. I'll stay. Come on."

She hesitated, reluctance furrowing her brow. Finally, she relented and carefully stood. "Okay. I'm sorry, Lily."

"Hey, it's fine. I've got work to do anyway." I nodded at my laptop bag that sat next to my chair. "Just yell out if you need anything."

"Will do. Thanks, lovey."

I gave her a hug. "Now go rest." Gee, that headache had come on suddenly, and Millicent was never one to complain, so it must have been painful.

After an hour of editing, it was time to check on her. After taking the tablets, she should be feeling a bit better. But maybe the pain had eased off, and she'd fallen asleep—goodness knew, she needed it.

I walked quietly to her room. The door was ajar, so I pushed it open enough to poke my head in. Millicent was lying on her side under the covers. Her eyes opened. She croaked out, "Hey."

That didn't sound good. "Is it still bad?"

"Ah huh. Worst headache I've ever had."

"Do you want me to call James?"

"No, no. They're short-staffed. He needs to work." I

wasn't going to argue with her—I'd just call him anyway. With the baby's due date so close, anything could go wrong.

"Just rest. I'll be back." I left her door open just in case she needed to call out. On returning to the kitchen, I slid my phone from my pocket and dialled James.

"Hey, Lily." He sounded tentative, and no wonder. He knew I was with Millicent and was probably wondering what was up. "Is everything okay?"

"I think so, but I'm not sure. Millicent is lying down with a massive headache. She took some paracetamol an hour ago, but it's done nothing. She didn't want me calling you, but I've never seen her so unwell. Do you think you could come get her, maybe take her to the doctor, just in case?"

"Definitely. I'll be there in five. And you did the right thing, Lily. I bet she told you not to bother me at work."

"Yep. I love her, hence why I didn't listen. Anyway, get your behind here ASAP." We hung up, and I breathed out a relieved sigh. James would come home, and everything would be fine.

I walked to the French doors and gazed out to the cold wetness beyond. I wrapped my arms around myself and shivered. Was the snake group out there, just waiting for us to make a mistake? And was Millicent really okay? I didn't know much about pregnancy, but a severe headache couldn't be a good sign, could it? One of the dogs padded over and nuzzled my hand for a pat. I stroked his head. "You're a sweetie, aren't you? You know when we humans need a hug. Clever boy."

Footsteps came from the living room, and I turned as

James strode into the kitchen, Beren close behind. Pepper wagged his tail and ran to James. He patted him, then looked at me, worry in his eyes. "Is she still lying down?"

"Yes. In your room."

He hurried past. Beren gave me a quick wave as he followed James into the bedroom. Some of the tension seeped from my shoulders—if anyone would know what to do, it would be Beren. Mill was in the best hands ever.

I sat back down in front of my laptop and stared at the picture on the screen. It needed a couple of tweaks, but my mind wasn't on the job—I was likely to make the photo worse rather than better. The smooth, capable, and kind aura of Beren's magic warmed my scalp. Hopefully Millicent would walk out with them sans headache.

I bit my fingernail. Waiting, waiting, always waiting. Didn't matter how much practice I got, I'd never get better at it. Finally, James came out. "Millicent has pre-eclampsia. There's nothing Beren can do here—it's complicated, and we don't want to risk trying to fix anything with magic now the baby is involved. We're taking her to hospital. I've called our midwife and told her we're on our way."

"Is she a witch?"

"Yes, although she usually does things the non-witch way. She calls on her magic in desperate situations. She can't perform too many miracles, or she's going to attract unwanted attention. If they can't treat Millicent effectively, she'll have a C-section."

"Make sure you let me know what's happening. Okay?" I really wanted to go with them, but they didn't need me in the way. "Let me say goodbye." Without waiting for his answer, I rushed into their room and to Millicent, who was sitting up, grimacing. "Good luck, Mill. I hope you feel better soon, and I'll be looking forward to the news of the little one, whenever that happens." I bent down and gave her a hug.

"Thanks, Lily. And thanks for calling James. Turns out, this is dangerous, and I really do need to go to hospital. They tell you about pre-eclampsia in the antenatal classes, but I just thought I had a normal headache. If we don't treat it, the kidneys start to shut down, and the baby and I could die." Her brow furrowed, and she placed both hands protectively over her baby bump.

"But it won't get to that, sweetheart." James kissed her forehead.

I stood, and James helped Millicent to her feet. I gave them a despondent wave. "See you guys later."

Millicent gave me a wan smile. "James will let you know when the baby's out. It might still be a few days. Apparently they try and manage your blood pressure to start with."

"Bye, Lily," said Beren as he made a doorway and stepped through. James made one for him and Mill, and then they were gone too, leaving me alone. A cold wetness touched my hand. I jumped. Sheesh! Pepper. So, I wasn't alone. I smiled. "Mummy will be home before you know it, and you'll have a new little one to watch over." Both dogs wagged their tails. "Yep, everything will be just fine." My voice sounded thin in the empty room. Okay, so the room wasn't exactly empty, but it felt like it now that everyone had left.

My phone rang. News already? My heart raced as I slid the phone out of my pocket. But it was Will. "Hey."

"Hey, Lily. Are you okay?"

"Not really. I mean, *I'm* fine, but things aren't the best." I explained what had happened.

"She's in good hands. Don't worry."

I blew out a breath. "Yeah, yeah, I know, but I'm still going to worry."

"Well, I've got something that might take your mind off it for a few hours."

"Oh, and what would that be?"

"We're going back to Dover."

"Why? I mean, not that I mind—I could do with a walk in the *refreshing* sea air." And by refreshing, I meant bloody freezing. It might take my mind off everything.

"There's been two more jumpers. I called the police to check in about whether they found out who that woman was. I told them I worked for the Kent police. They wouldn't tell me the woman's name, but they let spill that they'd had two more since that time. Another woman in her sixties, and a man in his twenties. That's too many suicides, even for this time of year."

"What's the time of year got to do with it?"

"During winter, when there's less daylight, we have more suicides. I won't go into the science behind it, but suffice it to say, it's a fact. So, you okay to come? I need photographs, see if we can identify everyone. I have a feeling something's going on, and the police down there aren't giving me anything. Since there's been no magic detected—not that they've probably looked—it's not a PIB matter."

"Yeah, sure. Are we driving down again?" It was drizzling outside, and as much as I enjoyed checking out my English surrounds, I hated being on the road in bad weather. Travelling had made a wimp out of me.

"No. Travel to the PIB, and then we'll travel from here. We'll go to a Dover public toilet and call an Uber."

"You're such a romantic. I swear, you take me to the best toilets." I snorted. Back in April, on my twenty-fourth birthday, if someone had said I would become an expert in English public toilets, I would have laughed and laughed. Hmm. What a thing to be knowledgeable about. Unfortunately, it wasn't something I could put on my resumé.

"I try. I'm glad you appreciate it." The grin came across in his voice. "I'll see you soon. Bye."

"Bye." I checked my phone. The battery was at 80 percent—more than enough to take photos with. I magicked my laptop back home before magicking my thick coat and beanie to myself. Right, that was everything. Oh, no it wasn't. I held out my hand, and a fold-away umbrella appeared in it. *Now* I was ready. Ha! I'd master this being-prepared thing yet.

I patted the dogs goodbye and promised to be back later to feed them if James couldn't. It was a quick hop to the PIB, and then Will made a doorway for both of us to go to the public toilet. Seriously, how had this become my life? And the toilets were smaller and stinkier than normal. I gagged as I pushed the door open and hurried outside. I flicked open my umbrella to keep the steady but light rain off my head while Will ordered the Uber. Thankfully, it arrived within two minutes. The drive to the walking track took less than five minutes. The two-mile trek along the path wasn't pleasant, but at least we were walking quickly, so it didn't take long to warm up.

We reached the place where that lady had jumped from the other day. Will stopped and stared out to sea, the bottom of his black coat jagged by the wind and fluttering behind his legs. He was rather majestic, standing there with his dark hair blown back from his face, defined jaw hard set, and his serious green-grey gaze matching the colour of the agitated water. If he were an animal, he'd be a wild stallion. Was I being weird? I smiled to myself. Probably, but it was hard not to admire his beauty, even in such tragic circumstances.

A trickle of his magic prickled my skin. It added to the eeriness of being somewhere that so many people had died, and only recently too. I shuddered and asked, "Whatcha doing?"

"Feeling for traces of power. There's something faint in the air, kind of like a scent of perfume a couple of days after someone has visited. It's not strong enough to reveal a signature, but something's happened here, maybe even just the dissipation of a spell."

"So someone cast a spell somewhere else, and it died here? As in the spell, not the person, although maybe they did too."

"Yes." He swung his gaze from the cliff edge to me. "I

need you to try and get photos of the last two people who jumped off—preferably of their faces."

"Okay. I'll try." I handed him my umbrella, which he dutifully held over my head while I took my phone out and switched it to photo mode. I pointed it towards where the woman had been walking from last time we were here. If there was any similarity in cases, maybe they would all have arrived here the same way. "Show me the face of the last person to jump off the cliff." I had zero desire to get too close to the cliff, and if I wasn't specific, my magic was likely to show me the back of the person about to jump.

A young rake of a man with long limbs was frozen in time about twelve metres away, walking along the path towards me. He was dressed warmly in a grey puffy jacket and beanie. His expression was set to determined. I stepped closer to see his face more clearly. I stopped when I'd almost reached him and took another photo. His pinked cheeks and dark eyes gave nothing away, except maybe there was a lack of focus in his gaze, which jarred with the confident posture as he strode along and the clenched jaw which showed small bunched muscles. He was purposeful in every way, except his eyes told a different story. Maybe I was reading too much into things.

Just to make sure this was the right person, I lowered my phone, then raised it again, pointing it towards the cliff. "Show me the man who jumped off just before he jumped." I had no desire to see him take that final step. He appeared at the edge of safety, his back to me. How long had he stood there before he'd jumped? What had been going through his mind? What had made him forfeit the rest of his life? My heart pulsed with waves of sadness. What a waste—so much ahead of him, yet it wasn't enough to keep him here. I snapped two shots and turned to Will. "One down, one to go."

"Are you okay?" His brow furrowed in his signature move.

"Yeah. He was just so young. Maybe younger than me." I shook my head. "It's not right." There was nothing else to say, so I turned towards where I'd seen the man coming from, and I lifted my phone. "Show me the face of the second-last person who jumped off the cliff."

A woman in vibrant colours appeared on the path. Her bright-pink scarf actually looked quite festive contrasted with her white coat, which had peacock feathers printed all over it. She'd paired this with teal-blue jeans. She was quite the trendsetter. Her clothes were at odds with the vacant look on her face. The lipstick she wore would have been more at home on upturned lips, but she didn't bear her smile. Celebratory her outfit might have been, but her demeanour was anything but. I took a couple of close-ups of her face. Looking into her blue eyes coaxed a slither of goosebumps along my arms.

She would have been gorgeous in her younger years, although her beauty was still more than a shadow of its former self. The skin was pulled tight over high cheekbones, and her lips were full. The wrinkles at the sides of her eyes only emphasized that she was someone who loved to laugh. Her nose was super narrow and almost pointy on the end. I guessed nobody was perfect. I wasn't one to care what someone looked like, but her nose did look a bit strange. Had she had plastic surgery? That would explain her tight facial skin. Anyway, each to their own. Maybe she'd suffered with a huge nose, and it was something that had really affected her enjoyment of life. I took another photo, asked for the about-to-jump picture, hurriedly took it, then gave my phone to Will and took possession of my umbrella.

He didn't say anything while scrolling through the pictures. He airdropped them from my iPhone to his iPhone and gave me back my phone. Will looked around. "Okay, I guess we're good to go."

I perused our surroundings. "From here?"

"Yes. I know we're out in the open, but there's no one here. I'll meet you back at the PIB. You go first." He was always looking out for me. I gave him a quick kiss on the lips, made my doorway, and left. Unfortunately, I couldn't get the two faces out of my head. Even if there was no link to magic, the world had lost two precious souls. Thinking of those two souls made me think of another two—Millicent and the baby. I had to believe they would both be okay. Rather than worry, I should be excited because soon I'd get to hold my adorable, cuddly niece or nephew. The alternative didn't bear thinking about.

But I thought it anyway.

CHAPTER 4

An hour after we returned to the PIB, Ma'am called a meeting. Will, Liv, Imani, and I sat around the conference-room table, looking at Ma'am, who occupied her usual head-of-the-table spot. She held up three large photographs in one hand, fanned out as if they were a hand of cards. "These are our three suicide victims." She lay the pictures face up on the table, one by one. They were head shots of the deceased. One of them was from the internet—the woman Will and I had seen that day—as the death had been reported by the media. The other two were close-ups of the photos I'd taken. The background was indistinct and almost out of frame. Ma'am had made sure of it, so if anyone else saw the pictures, they wouldn't think them unusual and ask how we'd come across photos of the victims from Dover. Someone had written each person's name on their photo.

Ma'am looked at Liv. "Thank you for digging through the police reports in the system and clarifying their names."

Liv smiled. "Always a pleasure, Ma'am." This thing where Liv worked partly for the Kent police and partly for the PIB was a boon for us. We could always call in some favours from our contacts in the police, but this was easier, faster, and more discreet.

Ma'am folded her arms and leaned back in her chair. "Before the first suicide, there hadn't been a suicide there for a month. There were two accidental deaths two weeks before, though. In any case, this cluster of deaths is curious at the very least. There is nothing at this stage tying them together, and we have no proof that they were magically induced."

"So why are we investigating them, then?" I asked. It was a fair question, especially considering how short-staffed the PIB was. I wasn't an expert, but it looked as if those people had jumped because they'd wanted to. Even if their eyes had shown reluctance or an almost trancelike state, I had no idea what someone felt when they were in that moment of despair and hopelessness. It wasn't as if anyone had pushed them, unless it was a spell kind of like the one Owen the Oracle had cast. Were these people dying so someone else benefitted—for an inheritance, or so another person could get their job? Nah, that would be too much of a coincidence, wouldn't it?

"Because Will has a hunch, dear, and he's never been wrong. In fact, I would call his hunches a talent."

How did I not know this about him? "Did you know this, Liv?"

She furrowed her brow. "What, that Will has a knack for sniffing out a magical crime?"

"Yes."

She shrugged. "I suppose so. He's sniffed out a couple of crimes that the rest of us had no idea about, at least while I've been on duty. If Will thinks magic is involved, I'd be inclined to believe it."

I eyed Imani. "And you?" She smirked and nodded. I folded my arms. "Fine. I guess we can continue." Why was I always the last to know everything? It was a bad habit that I didn't appreciate. And, for the record, I was paying attention; I always paid attention… well, mostly… when I wasn't in my own world.

Ma'am raised her brow. "Honestly, Lily, it's not as if we keep things from you on purpose. You need to pay more attention. Now, let's stop this nonsense and get back to what we were discussing." She dismissed me by shifting her gaze to the other side of the table—to Will and Imani. My cheeks heated. What was I even doing here? I should be hunting more photography work. I wasn't an agent, and with just about every case they got me to work on, I failed in some way and came across as an idiot. Maybe I *was* an idiot? Will gave me a sympathetic look, his lips pressed together, head cocked to the side. I sighed quietly and looked back at Ma'am.

"We unfortunately don't have access to the bodies, so we're going to have to investigate this the hard way—by interviewing the family and friends of the deceased. Because they would have been told suicide was the cause, they would be suspicious of additional police questioning them, and we don't want to alarm them or give them cause to think anything else is afoot. Also, even though Will has never had a wrong hunch, there's a first time for everything, so it's best we're subtle. In this regard, I've come up with a plan." She lifted her chin slightly and smiled proudly. Of course she'd go with a dramatic pause before the big reveal. She really should have her own reality TV show. "Because Imani and Will look too much like agents, and I don't want to compromise Olivia's work with the police, I'm sending you, Lily." She smiled, but it didn't warm my heart.

"I can't go. I'll stuff it up. Seriously. And who am I supposed to be if I'm not police or an agent?"

"You're writing an article on suicides at the White Cliffs and contributing to research on suicide in general. You can say that you're focussing on how many people give any indication as to their state of mind or seek help in the weeks before taking their own lives. It means we can ask questions about their recent activity, see if there's any kind of connection."

"But what if they don't want to talk to me? And what if me bringing it up causes them more heartache, and it turns out all this is for nothing?" I hated lying at the best of times, but lying to grieving people at the worst possible time in their lives? That was just low.

She raised a steely brow. "But what if they were coerced somehow and actually murdered? If that's the case, they deserve justice, not to mention, we need to stop whoever's doing this."

"If, indeed, someone is," I countered. She did have a good point, but since I was only just learning of Will's hunches, how did I know they really were super fabulous? Angelica could be overstating his ability just to get me on board.

"I'd like you to record the conversations. Just let them know you're recording them—it's standard procedure for this kind of thing, so it won't seem unusual. Agent Jawara can go with you and wait nearby. I won't leave you without protection, and that leads me to another topic: Regula Pythonissam. I want to arrange another meeting to discuss the new information James unearthed because of the photos you took the other night. But now Millicent is in hospital, it will have to wait."

I chewed on my top lip. Could I say no to interviewing people? Surely there was an agent who could do it, someone who looked inconspicuous? Will cleared his throat. I looked at him. He had his head tilted and was looking at me like "don't you dare say no." I folded my arms and stared at him like, "I'll do whatever the hell I want." He shook his head slowly and firmly. I lifted my chin.

Imani slapped the table, and I jumped. "For goodness' sake, Lily. Just do it. We need you. If there was anyone else Ma'am thought suitable who wasn't already busy, she would've put them on the job. You'll be fine, and I can vouch for Will's hunches. I'll go over the questions you'll need to ask. It'll be fine; think of it as helping people rather than making things worse for them."

Beaten into submission, I narrowed my eyes one last time, just to make sure everyone got that I wasn't exactly happy about this. "Fine. But only because I'm trusting you're right. If I hurt these people for no good reason, I'm going to be beyond unhappy."

Ma'am scrutinized me as if sizing up a reluctant dog that needed a bath. "Maybe you really aren't cut out for this work. Have I underestimated your emotional fortitude?"

"I daresay you have. I don't like hurting people. Just because it's to help them, doesn't mean I have to like it."

"None of us do, dear, but we stomach it and become hardened to it because there is no other way. In order to make differences that matter, sacrifice is required, but it will always be worth it. What is the price of sleeping at night?"

I could have answered "too high," but was it ever? For a lot of people, it probably was. Police and medical personnel sure had a hard time of it, even though they did the best they could. None of us could save everyone, no matter what we did, and sometimes the price was way too high—not everyone who did the right thing made it out alive, whether by choice somewhere like the White Cliffs of Dover or in the line of duty through no choice of their own. But for me? Questioning these people was not going to give me nightmares. My conscience would be bruised but not irrevocably damaged. "In this instance, the price is not very much, considering. I'll do the best I can. I promise."

"That's my girl. I'll let you set up your own appointments. Liaise with Olivia, gather as much information as you can, then let Agent Jawara know. Make those appointments as soon as you can." Ma'am looked at Will. "I'd like to see you at those funerals with a no-notice spell activated. None of the potential victims are witches, so you shouldn't attract attention. Just have a cover story ready in case they were inadvertently friends with a witch. See if you can find out anything, but I want subtlety."

Despite the fact that Ma'am was likely telling Will stuff he already knew, his poker face stayed intact as he nodded with grave seriousness, his forehead furrows on display. Will looked across the table at Liv. "Can you check at the end of each day to see if anyone else has jumped and let me know? If we have any other jumpers, I'll take Lily out there to get more photos." He shot me a "sorry" look. I shrugged. What else could I do but go along with what they wanted?

"Will do," said Liv.

Ma'am slid the pictures across the table to Olivia, then stood. "You ladies can deal with these. I'm off to another meeting. Stay safe, everyone, and I'll see you all back here when you've done your jobs." She glanced at her watch. "Which I imagine will be in a couple of days." She looked at Will. "Keep me updated." Without waiting for an answer, she left the non-witch way, via the door.

Imani stood. "Lily, I've got a few things to finish. Call me when you're ready to make those appointments, and we'll block out some times that suit."

"Okay."

"See you all later." She made a doorway and stepped through.

Will turned to me. "I'll see you both later as well, likely tonight at home. I should be there for dinner."

I smiled. "Sounds good."

We all stood and headed for the door. Outside, Liv and I went one way, and Will another. Liv and I grabbed a coffee and tea from the cafeteria, then headed to her office. As we entered, I frowned and chewed my fingernail. This was also Millicent's office. "I wonder how they're doing." I took a seat at Liv's desk. She sat next to me and fired up her computer.

"I'd say they're okay. Maybe there's just been no change, and they're waiting? I'm sure James will call or message when he has any news."

"Have you heard anything from B?"

She shook her head. "I'll let you know if I do. Come on. Thinking about it won't help, and we've got work to do."

While Liv researched the people who'd died, I magicked my laptop to myself and started researching suicide and depression, making a list of questions for the family and friends. If I was supposed to be researching it, I should know what I was talking about. We'd been at it for ages.

I looked up. Darkness blacked out beyond the window, and the office light reflected off the glass. My stomach grumbled. The top right corner of my laptop screen read 5:04 p.m. "We missed lunch and afternoon tea. No wonder I'm starving." My stomach gurgled again, but then a rush of adrenaline swooshed through it, dampening my hunger. I still hadn't heard anything from James.

Frowning, I grabbed my phone and sent him a message.

Hey, wondered how everyone was doing. Is Millicent okay? Has her headache gone? Xx

Within two minutes, my phone dinged. Thank God.

Sorry, Lily, just been caught up here, making sure Mill and the baby are okay. The doctor's given her some blood-pressure medication, and her headache's a bit better. The baby is okay at this stage, but we're closely monitoring the situation. If things get worse, we'll have to induce, but, hopefully, we can keep the pre-eclampsia at bay for a few more days. I'll message you later xx.

Okay, thanks for letting me know. Sorry to bother you. Send Mill my love xx.

He sent back a smiley face. I updated Liv. "That's fantastic news. See, I knew she'd be okay. She's in great hands. I just have a bit more to do; then we can go. Give me another ten minutes?"

"Yeah, sure." I typed in *Westerham Events* to see what was coming up out and about. Every now and then, something fantastic would be on, something that was part of the experience of being here and being part of the community, like the Christmas-tree display at the church. Hmm, not exactly what I had in mind—a local plastic-surgery place, Changing Faces, was having its first-year anniversary party next Saturday. Dr Joe Ezekal had moved his successful practice from London to Westerham a year ago because, as he put it, "There was a real need in this vibrant community for my services." What, were we uglier down here compared to

London, or had everyone in London done everything they could do, and he needed fresh meat? I wasn't that hard up for stuff to do that I needed to go there. Right, what else was on?

Hmm, this looked all right. The local art gallery—yes, the one that Patrick and his parents ran—had changed hands and was having a showing of a famous Spanish nature photographer. Ooh, that looked awesome. It was also next Saturday. Done. It'd been ages since I'd wandered through an exhibition. I smiled. Such a small thing, but I was really looking forward to it.

"Okay, I'm done. Just have to wait for this stuff to print; then we can go." The printer zipped to life with the click and suck of paper being loaded.

"Great. Hey, are you free next Saturday?"

"I think so, unless B has made plans for us that I don't know about. Why?" I told her about the photography exhibition. "Oh, wow, yes. I'd love to. Count me in."

I grinned. "Awesome. We'll see if B and Will are free too; then maybe we can grab a high tea or something afterwards."

Liv laughed. "Always with the food. You're hilarious."

"Well, everyone has to eat. Might as well enjoy it since we're doing it anyway."

Once everything printed, we had a decent pile of paper. Liv handed the wad to me. "You'll need to read all this before you interview everyone. Obviously, you'll have to ask questions to answers you already know because we don't want them knowing how much you've researched their loved ones, or it'll look weird. But for you to know which directions to take your questioning, you'll need to know their background. Is that cool?"

"Is there a speed-reading spell?"

She looked at me like "what?" "Why in all that's witchy would you ask me? I'm not exactly the expert."

Oops. That was a slight sore spot for Liv. She wished she could cast spells like the rest of us. I imagined it was frustrating since she hung out with us all the time. Not that she complained, but this was the third or fourth comment over the last few months that she'd made on the topic. "Sorry. Maybe there's a spell that allows non-witches to become witches?"

"Ha! If that were possible, why wouldn't witches just make everyone like them, and then there'd be no need to hide."

"Yeah, but wouldn't that create more problems? There's so many horrible people in the world, and then they'd have more power to do evil."

"True. Anyway, despite my intermittent disappointment, I'm fine." She smiled. "But, seriously, I'm the last person you should ask about anything witchy."

"Okay. But you work with them now. You're around more of them than I am." I laughed.

"Hmm, true. Okay, Miss Witch, you going to take me home?"

"Yes, my lady. After you." I made my doorway and followed its outline with my finger so Liv could see where it was. She stepped through carefully, so as not to have anything accidentally chopped off—doorways could be deadly—and I followed.

Once home, Liv ran up to shower, and I plonked myself in an armchair in front of the fire and read through the sheets on all the victims, if that's what they were. The first woman, the lady we'd seen in person, was Emily Armand. Originally born in France, she moved to London with her French husband and two young children when she was in her late twenties. Her kids were now in their forties. Emily and her husband, Bertrand, divorced ten years ago. Emily had worked as a hairdresser before retiring five years ago. She'd owned a successful salon in London. Wow. She must've had a lot of money. But with all this good stuff, other than the divorce, why kill yourself? Was she suffering depression? There was nothing on her file about seeing the doctor for anything other than routine check-ups over the years, at least not that we'd found, but I would imagine not everything was on file. Maybe we'd need magic to access other records later, after talking to her family.

The next picture was Andrew Porter. He was twenty-three and lived at home with his parents and two younger siblings. Liv had pulled his school records. Private-school education, average results, apparently a quiet, pleasant, and happy kid at school. There had been a couple of instances of bullying, and he'd attended school counselling. Being confidential, Liv obviously couldn't access what the counselling had been about. That was definitely a question I'd need to ask. Had he been depressed? If so, there was no reason for us to be investigating his death, was there? He was attending university to study linguistics, had a girlfriend and a gym membership. So, overall, it appeared that his life was going okay.

Person number three: Alice Baker. Successful fifty-nine-year-old fashion designer living in Surrey. Cohabitated with her female partner, travelled a lot for work, was known as being flamboyant and the life of the party. She'd even won a couple of fashion awards—Liv had printed the articles on them. Alice had had breast cancer and a double mastectomy five years ago and reconstructive surgery about a year ago. She was obviously a survivor, so why kill herself now? Had the cancer spread or returned? I eyed her photo again. Other than the glazed look in her eyes, everything looked as it should.

There were other minor details about the three. When I finished reading, I stared into the fire, giving my brain space to find any kind of pattern. But there was none. Every person was different, from having varying family backgrounds and jobs, to living in different places—even the two who lived in London lived in separate suburbs, seven miles apart. I sighed, frustration tightening my jaw. Were we wasting time? Maybe one person had been coerced into jumping, but the other two had chosen to? If that was the case, then trying to find links was a waste of time. But at what point would we know?

My phone rang, and, because I wouldn't be me if I didn't startle, I jumped. I swear I was going to have a heart attack one of these days. Would I be the first person to ever die from a phone call? I checked the screen. James! "Hey, how's everything going? Is Millicent okay? Do we have a baby?"

"She's fine, and no, no baby yet. She's still a week and a half from her due date, so if we can keep the baby in there a bit longer, it will be better. She's still stable, and the headache's gone. She had blood pressure of one fifty over one hundred, but they've gotten it down to one thirty over ninety. They're monitoring her every couple of hours, and they'll do more tests tomorrow. I just wanted you to know that I'm home, so you won't have to feed the pups. Unless Millicent calls me, I'm going to be here tonight. I'm going back to the hospital in the morning—there's nothing I can do there, and I need sleep."

"Fair enough. Thanks for letting me know. I'll fill everyone in. And if you need me for anything, let me know."

"Okay, thanks."

"How are you holding up?" My brother wasn't a super stress-head, but he cared deeply about his family. It would be a surprise to me if he managed to sleep much tonight.

"I'm okay. Worried, obviously, but she's got the best doctor and midwife you could possibly have. There's nothing else I can do except be ready for her when she needs me, so I'm trying not to panic." His nervous chuckle sounded almost manic.

"Do you want to come round here and have dinner with us tonight?"

"Nah. I'm going to eat something, watch TV, then get an early night. Thanks for asking."

"Not a problem. Well, good luck with sleeping, and again, if you need me…."

"Thanks, Lil. I'll talk to you tomorrow."

"Okay. Night. Love you."

"Night, love you too."

Shuffled footsteps at the door heralded Liv in her Ugg boots. She'd dressed in a comfy-looking black tracksuit that had bright-yellow sleeves and stripes down the side of the legs. "You're looking rather bumblebee this evening." I grinned.

She twirled. "You like? I snagged this at a sale the other day. Bzzz, bzzz."

I laughed. "It's cute. James just called. He's at home tonight, and Mill's still in hospital. They're keeping her in until the baby's born."

"Sounds reasonable."

I stood. "I've finished reading all this stuff. Why don't you help me cook some spag bol, and we can discuss what questions I should be asking?"

"Sounds good, but why don't you just, you know…" She waved her arms in the air, imitating spell casting.

"I could, but I feel like doing something non-witchy to pass the time. Doing everything with spells gives me a lot more free time, and I don't always know what to do with it since everyone works full-time, and I'm often by myself. I mean, we could sit here and discuss things, but I feel like doing something."

"Fair enough." She turned and led the way to the kitchen where we got prepping, chatting, and cooking.

When we finished, I wrote all the questions we'd decided on in my notebook.

"Done. The problem is setting up interviews. I know we want to get this done as soon as possible, but shouldn't we wait till after the funerals?"

"You're probably right. Their family and friends are probably still in shock too. I'd check with Angelica first, but you'll probably get more information out of them when they've had time to digest what's happened."

A knock sounded at the reception-room door, and Liv jumped up from the kitchen table. "I'll get it." I smiled. She was so cute being excited to see Beren. She returned with Beren and Will. It was my turn to jump up. The grin that lit up his face was irresistible. Those dimples were my kryptonite. I squished him in a huge hug.

"This is just a crazy guess, but I'm thinking you're happy to see me?" He chuckled.

"Always." I confirmed it with a kiss that had Liv making gagging noises.

"Get a room," Beren teased.

"Do you know the number of times we've had to put up with you two?" I turned and raised an eyebrow.

Beren smirked. "Good. As long as you've suffered more than me, that's okay."

The doorbell rang. Liv and I looked at each other and shrugged, which translated to, "Were you expecting anyone?" "No." "Were you?" "No." Right. Someone had to take charge. "I'll get it," I said.

As I exited the kitchen, Will was close behind. Although

I was pretty sure I didn't need protection, I let him come. I'd had enough arguing with people today, and it didn't matter. When I reached the door, I called out, "Who is it?" There was no answer.

Will said quietly, "Put up your RTS."

Huh? But then it sunk in—Return to Sender. I supposed it would make it easier if we had shorthand for this stuff, especially if we had to convey the message quickly. "Okay." I drew on my power and activated the spell, then opened the door.

Nothing. The front porch was empty. Hmm, actually, there was something there. I stepped outside and gazed down the driveway towards the street, but it was fairly dark, and I couldn't see much. Tiny, freezing needles of rain stabbed my face. Whoever had rung the doorbell was likely long gone, and I had no desire to run around the streets looking for them. I bent down and picked up the white envelope that had been left on the welcome mat. Hmm, *welcome* mat. A nicer way of saying "a mat you want people to wipe their feet on so they don't walk mud or dog poo through your house." Other than wiping your feet, there was nothing welcoming about a rough-textured rectangle on the ground outside one's house.

"Lily? What are you doing down there?"

Oh. I looked up at Will, who was gazing down at me with a perplexed expression. "Um, I got stuck on a thought."

He laughed and shook his head. "I should've known."

I stood and hurried inside. Despite my brain getting

sidetracked on the less-than-welcoming nature of welcome mats, I didn't miss the weird feeling the envelope gave me. It was a subtle vibration, almost like an electric shock. The forceful tingles against my fingers were creepy, and goosebumps paraded up my arms. Preoccupied with the envelope, I forgot to shut the door, but Will took care of it for me; the small thud followed by the click of the lock brought me back to the moment.

I held up the envelope. "Can you hold this and tell me if you feel anything unusual?"

His brows drew down. "Are you all right?"

"I'm fine, but I need to know if this is spelled or something. It feels strange to me. Almost like when someone casts a spell, but ickier and only what's touching it. Normally if someone is using magic, I feel it on my scalp or nape, but this is giving me weirdness on my fingertips. It's yucky, like running your fingers along a dry beach towel."

"I'm afraid I'm not too familiar with that sensation. Can't say I go to the beach much."

Ha, I forgot he lived in England and not Cronulla, where I was from. It was a lot hotter, and the beach had fun waves and soft, yellowish sand. Most of my summertime was spent at the beach, and every beach-going person knew the horrible feeling of dry fingers on dry towel, but I'd bet that some crazy people actually liked that sensation. I shuddered. "Can you just take the damn thing and tell me?" I shoved it into his hand.

"No need to get—" As soon as it settled into his palm, he scrunched his nose up and pressed his lips together. "Oh, you're right. It's been spelled. Hang on a sec." The firm rightness of Will's magic caressed my nape. I assumed he was looking at the envelope with his second sight, looking for the symbol that would indicate what kind of spell it was. Uneasiness tightened my stomach muscles. Finally, his magic stopped. "It's nothing much. Just a spell to let the sender know when the envelope's been opened."

"The icky feeling must be the signature feel of the magic of whoever sent it, or maybe they wanted to freak us out?"

"I can't usually tell the difference between different magic, Lily, so it must be intentional."

"Should we open it?" I eyed the innocuous whiteness in Will's hand. It was probably from whoever had sent me that card a while ago, the one that said they'd hoped I'd recovered and I was more valuable than I knew. They'd mentioned then that they intended we'd meet one day. Creepy.

Will's intense gaze flicked from the envelope to me. "Do we want to annoy whoever sent it? And how long can you go without knowing what's inside? It might even be from a friend."

My eyes executed a half roll, and I stared at the ceiling. Was Will trying to be dense? I let my eyeballs finish their roll because, well, it was satisfying, and I stared at him. "How many witches do I know? Not many, right? And the ones I do know have my mobile number. No witch is going to send me a letter. I'm betting it's from whoever sent me that card. And I would go so far as to say that whoever it is, is not a friend."

"That's a lot of assumptions, but I'm inclined to agree with you. I just wanted to know what you thought before I gave you advice."

"Since when does my opinion matter to anyone around here?" I folded my arms. Okay, so I might be getting a tad defensive, but he knew what I meant. I wasn't really trying to argue about it. This envelope was giving me a case of the heebie-jeebies. I made a bubble of silence. "Could it be from RP?"

"RP?"

"Yes, Regula Pythonissam. Since we're doing acronyms for spells, we may as well do it for them. That way, we won't always have to make bubbles of silence."

He nodded slowly. "Good idea. And yes, it could be from them. So, do you want to wait to open it? When I asked if you wanted to annoy whoever it was, I meant on purpose." He smirked. "If it is from them, I think we should take every opportunity to irritate them."

"Isn't that akin to poking the bear? Will it make them do something awful?"

"No, but it might make them so angry that they act without thinking. Maybe it will bring them out of hiding long enough for us to catch another one of them?" Will dropped the envelope on the small, semicircular entryway table sitting against the wall. "If that's what a dry hand running down a dry beach towel feels like, I don't want to ever do it."

Footsteps came down the hall. Liv and Beren appeared. Liv gave us a quick once-over, then asked, "Who was it?"

I shrugged. "They were gone by the time I opened the door. They left something behind, and it's spelled so they know when we open it. I guess they probably travelled away, but then again, how did they travel here?"

"Maybe they travelled to the toilet in the village and walked here?" said Liv.

I nodded. "I suppose so." As much as I loved the ease of travelling, it also worked against us when it came to bad guys. They could disappear and go wherever they wanted in seconds. It didn't make tracking them down very easy. Seemed like every positive had a negative in life. Wanted to be thin—you had to eat fewer double-chocolate muffins and run more. Working long hours meant earning more, but then you had less time to enjoy the money you'd earned. Having a dog would be awesome, but then there was poo to pick up.

I stared at the envelope. What if it was a warning I really should heed? But did I really want to read a threat? Then I'd just worry. But not knowing would be torture too. What if it wasn't even from Regula Pythonissam? There was no witch I could think of who'd send me a letter or card, but you never knew. What if one of my friends from Sydney was actually a witch and I didn't know? Nah, they'd just text me.

To open or not to open? I shut my eyes and turned my head so that when I opened my eyes, I would be looking somewhere other than at the tempting white package. My gaze ended up on Liv. "Why don't we have dinner. I'm starving." It had been hours since I'd eaten. I couldn't be expected to think clearly or make good decisions when hungry. My stomach was taking up at least 50 percent of my attention, if not more.

"Are you sure?" Will asked. It was a Tardis question: he was asking way more than just those three words. Am I sure I want to leave that thing unopened on the table and walk away? Am I sure I want to annoy whoever sent it by not opening it? How long could I go not knowing what the message was? I had no idea. The only thing I was sure about was that I needed to eat.

"I'm sure. I don't think I've ever made a good decision on an empty stomach, so I plan to eat first and think later. Come on." I headed to the kitchen.

"The procrastination is strong in this one." Beren chuckled from behind me.

"At least I'm good at something." I grinned.

Liv sat at the table. "What you're also good at is cooking. This smells amazing."

"You helped."

"Yeah, but it was your recipe. I just stirred the pot and chopped up some onion, parsley, and garlic."

Once we were all seated, the spaghetti in a huge bowl in the middle of the table, I drew a trickle of power and waved my hand over the bowl as if I were a magician. "Please heat the food we are about to eat." The food started steaming as I sat back, rather proud of myself. But the plume of vapour thickened and poured towards the ceiling. Heat radiated from the bowl, and then it cracked in half, each half falling outwards, spilling food over the edges onto the table. Oh crap. What had I done? It wasn't supposed to keep heating!

Will's power tickled my scalp, and the haze coming off the food dissipated. He looked up at me with a "you idiot" expression on his face. "You need to be specific, Lily. How many times do we have to tell you? You've pretty much nuked dinner."

Liv and Beren looked at each other, trying not to laugh. Then we all stared at the mess of desiccated meat and hard, stiff pasta. It was practically mummified. Shame warmed my neck and cheeks. "Oops. Can you magic it back to how it was?"

Will shook his head. "Too difficult. I'd have to specify how much water to put back. I'm sorry."

I sighed. I'd actually spent a lot of time making it. Next time, I'd use the microwave to reheat dinner. I had no finesse—I was finesseless. And yes, I did just make up a word because there weren't enough in the world. "Finesseless."

Liv's brows drew down. "What?"

I smiled. "Just making up a word. It's fun to say. Finesseless. Try it."

Liv giggled. "Finesseless. Ooh, you're right. Finesseless. Why don't you guys try it rather than sitting there with such silly faces?"

I laughed. Will and Beren were shaking their heads, and Will was circling his finger in the air around his ear, suggesting we were nuts. My stomach gurgled, and everyone stared at me. Trust my stomach to remind me of what was important. "So what are we going to do for dinner then? I think we have some lamb chops in the freezer." I tried not to think of how cute the lamb would have been, frolicking around until its little life was cut short. Gah, now I felt bad.

"What do you feel like?" Beren asked. "We'll just get some Witcheroo. What about pizza?"

We all agreed and chose toppings, but after the food arrived, while we ate, my thoughts kept dashing down the hallway to the table in the entry and that standard white envelope that contained a not-so-standard message. Who was it from, and what did it say? But most of all: Did I really want to know?

Damn. Yes. Yes, I wanted to know. I hated surprises, and that message was a surprise waiting to happen. Hmm, was it still a surprise if I knew it was waiting for me? I was going to go with yes. I stood.

Will looked at me. "You couldn't wait, could you?"

"Nope. I suppose they'll learn I have no patience. I just hope they can't use that knowledge against me later." Now that I'd made up my mind, I just wanted it over and done with. I hurried to the entry hall, and, despite my spaghetti-heating disaster, I channelled my magic as I didn't want to touch the creepy envelope. "Please open this envelope and gently place what's inside on my hand." I made sure to be specific because I didn't want my hand sliced in half with a wicked paper cut. That would be my luck.

Liv stood next to me and stared at the paper floating into my palm. It landed, and I tensed, my fingers splayed rigid, as if I were holding a spider. The eerie vibration was gone, but I still feared what the note said. As I unfolded it,

Will put his large, warm hand on my shoulder, and Beren said, "Whatever it is, we're here for you."

"Thanks." My heart beat faster. The neat script was in the same hand as the previous note. I read the letter aloud.

"Dearest Lily,

I hope this missive finds you well. This is just a little note to remind you that I am always watching, and, soon, I will invite you to stay with me. I'm eager to meet you and see what amazing things we can achieve together. If even half the things your mother told me about you are true, there will be nothing we can't do. I should warn you, though, that there are those who don't want us to collaborate. It would be a shame if anything were to happen to you before we could meet. So heed my warning, and watch your back. Excuse the cliché, but that was the most apt phrase for the situation.

Until we finally meet…"

Silence. It was as if the atmosphere coagulated while we processed the words. In my head, I heard the evil "Mwahahahahahaha" tacked onto the end of the message. *Were they always watching?* The hairs on my nape stood, and I gave in to the urge to gaze around the entryway, looking for hidden cameras. I engaged my other sight to check for anything hidden with magic. Nope, nothing. I breathed out loudly.

Will squeezed my shoulder. "Why don't we go and sit in the living room where it's warmer. Here, give me the note. I'd like to read it again." I turned and handed it to him, then followed Liv and Beren into my favourite room in the house. Even though there were only two chairs next to the fire, I headed for one anyway and sat. I needed the comforting warmth of the flames.

There was so much to unpack. My university teachers had loved that phrase. "Let's unpack this text." If only I was back at uni, living a life that didn't include witches and deaths and special agents. My stomach somersaulted as if I were on a rollercoaster.

They had known my mother.

She had spoken to them about me.

I gripped the chair arms and snapped my head back, purposefully thudding it into the soft chair back a couple of times. What had Mum said? How well did she know this person? Were they even telling the truth?

Will knelt in front of my chair and grabbed my hand. "Hey, look at me." I stared down into his loving eyes. They were a stunning Prussian blue in the subdued light. He squeezed my hand. "There's a lot to process. Let's take some time to think it through, and then we'll talk about it. That warning feels like a faux warning—if that person is so concerned, why don't they just tell you exactly who you should be worried about? Whoever sent this wants to unsettle you, frighten you, keep you off balance, but we won't let them. We're not going to give them that power over you. We're all here for you, and I'll die before I let anything happen to you. Okay?"

I nodded, not trusting myself to speak. Stupid tears lurked in the back of my throat and behind my eyeballs. The slightest movement would set them off, and I hated crying in front of people. I bit my tongue as a distraction. Liv placed her hand on my arm. "Do you have any idea who it might be?"

I shook my head. "Should we see if James got one too? I mean, I'm not the only awesome person in the family. And if it's true… that Mum knew this person, they would know all about James too." Then something struck me. "But Mum couldn't have known how strong our magic would be or what talents we'd have. So what could she possibly have told this person that would have any relevance to anything?"

Beren stood behind Liv and looked down at me. "If he —I'm going to assume it's a *he*—has been watching you, he'll have some inkling that your magic is strong because, yeah, your mother couldn't have known what kind of witch you'd be."

"But no one outside us knows what my talents are." We'd been careful, but what if we hadn't been careful enough?

Will dropped my hand and sat on the floor cross-legged. "Think about it, Lily. You've been involved in some pretty intense magical battles lately. And, if it's who I think it is, they might have seen your magic display at the warehouse the night you saved me. And don't disregard all the information Dana managed to gather before we knew she'd gone rogue."

I sighed, my shoulders drooping. "So you think it's RP?"

Liv looked at me and scrunched her forehead. "Who's RP?"

I went to make a bubble of silence, then realised the one I'd made earlier was still up. I was so efficient that I deserved a pat on the back. It must also mean my magic was stronger than I thought. I wasn't even feeling tired from holding a spell for ages, albeit a spell that didn't use too much power. All my magic use over the past few weeks was paying off. "Regula Pythonissam. Will and I decided to shorthand their name. Then, if we forget to put up a bubble of silence, they likely won't know we're talking about them. Plus, it's easier than saying their full name."

"Hmm, I like it."

Beren looked at Will. "What do you want to do now?"

"Get the note and envelope to the lab and have them analysed. Who knows; there may be a magical signature left on the envelope or DNA. I also think having a chat with Angelica wouldn't hurt."

I rubbed my forehead. Had my mother been friends with this person, or had she been investigating them? I stopped mid forehead rub. "Will, who do you think it is?"

"Someone in RP. Either Dana or her boyfriend, the one involved in the tea debacle. From what I could gather, he's pretty high up in the food chain in the group—not that I was privy to much, but that's the impression I got before they decided I wasn't really there because I loved Dana." He clenched his jaw, hardness glinting in his eyes.

It warmed my heart that he only felt anger when he thought about her, but due to current circumstances, I didn't have time to soak in it and enjoy as if it were a deep, hot bubble bath. "Do you know who he really is?" I asked.

"He goes by two names: Achilles Pappas and Boss. Obviously, Boss is a nickname, but there's practically no information on his other name. I doubt Achilles Pappas is his real name. When we did background checks after the tea incident, the information was too bland and sparse, as if it were planted. We just found the basics: birth certificate, schools, tax file number, parents' address, but that was it. No place of work, no fixed address, no tax information. He doesn't claim government benefits either."

Why did none of that surprise me? "In other words, a slippery snake."

Will nodded. "Other than doing more research and checking in with Angelica, there's nothing more to do about this, Lily. As far as I'm concerned, nothing's changed—we'll still be extra careful with your safety and keep investigating your parents' disappearance and RP. I don't think you can be on your guard any more than you already are, plus, if you act as normally as possible, it will annoy the hell out of them, I bet." His cheeky grin made me think that maybe everything would be okay.

More fool me.

CHAPTER 5

Tossing, turning, and nightmares were not conducive to having a restful night, but at least I was able to sleep in. When I finally dragged myself out of bed, it was eleven. As usual, Will, Liv, and Angelica were already at work. I magicked my clothes on, went downstairs with my laptop, and sat at the kitchen table, then magicked myself a coffee. The only things I had to do today were editing photos and waiting for James to call. Today would only turn out to be memorable in a good way if Mill had the baby and everyone was well.

It was pouring outside and a chilly five degrees Celsius. As much as I had a lot on my mind, it was a great day to be inside working. Within two hours, I'd finished the photo edits and emailed them to my client. That was one job out of the way, but now I had nothing to do. Until those funerals were done, I couldn't interview anyone. Hmm, even though Mill wasn't well, maybe she'd be up for a visitor. From what James said, she didn't have a headache anymore. Plus, maybe he needed a break and would be happier leaving if someone else was with her.

I pulled out my phone and texted him. His reply came back in moments, and it was in the affirmative, plus it included the hospital coordinates, ward, and room number. Yes! I magicked my laptop up to my room and my coat to myself. After making my doorway, I pictured the coordinates James had sent and stepped through… into an occupied cubicle.

My eyes widened, as did those of the elderly lady sitting on the toilet. Oh, God. Her mouth dropped open. She stared at me. I stared at her. She stared. I stared. A trickle of wee echoed from her toilet, taking things from awkward and frightening to mortifying. And then she… well… blurted a trumpet noise, but not with a trumpet, or her mouth. Her eyes widened even further, as if she were surprised by it, and maybe she was. God knew, she wouldn't be the only one.

I wanted to say sorry, but if I spoke, it would make me more concrete. Maybe if I just opened the door and left, she'd think I was a hallucination or something. Also, there was no way anyone would believe her. I gave her a quick half smile, turned, and let myself out.

How the hell had that happened? Bloody James. He must have gotten something wrong, or maybe the woman had ignored the Out of Order sign and used the wrong toilet. I hadn't thought to check if the sign was still there because, well, I wasn't hanging around a nanosecond longer than I had to.

I practically jogged down the sterile hallways, following signs until I reached the maternity ward. The woman guarding the nurses' station asked me who I was looking for before I could sneak past. "I'm here to see Millicent Bianchi."

"She's in room 206, down that way." She pointed to my right.

"Thanks." The door was open, but I knocked anyway. "Hello."

"Come on in." James stood next to Mill's bed, and another man, slightly older-looking than James, sat in one of the two chairs next to her bed. He had straight, side-parted sandy brown hair in a neat cut. He wore a blue shirt and houndstooth jacket. "This is Millicent's cousin Daniel. Daniel, this is my sister, Lily."

He stood and gave me a half bow. "Pleased to meet you, Lily. I've heard so much about you, and, yes, it's all been good." He gave a short laugh.

"Lovely to meet you, Daniel." What a nice cousin he was, visiting Millicent even before the baby arrived. My sister-in-law had a moderately puffy face. Her usually prominent cheekbones were semi-hidden. I'd looked up preeclampsia, and swelling was a symptom, not to mention, pregnancy seemed to be a water-retentive kind of time.

I approached her bed. "How are you feeling?"

She sighed. "Tired and ready to get this baby out.

Hospital is so boring. If it wasn't for security issues, I'd get some work sent to me."

Daniel smiled. "Anything exciting happening in spy land?"

James chuckled. "Never." He winked.

"You guys are no fun. You never tell me anything." Daniel frowned.

Mill shook her head. "It's just a dangerous job and boring at times. You're not missing out on anything, you know."

Daniel slumped back in his chair. "I know. It's just, accountancy is so booooring. Can you talk about any cases that are over and done with?"

"Only bits and pieces, but here's not the place." James turned to me. "I'm just going to grab some food. Are you okay here, or do you want to come?"

"I came to see my gorgeous sister-in-law, so I'll stay here." I smiled. "Off you go. Take a break; get some fresh air."

James laughed. "What, you want me to enjoy the freezing rain outside? We're not in Sydney, you know."

"Oops, I forgot. Oh well, get some exercise by doing a few laps of the hallways." I stuck my tongue out at him.

He laughed. "Yeah, sounds like fun." He looked at Millicent. "Do you want anything?"

"Unless you can take this baby out right now, then no."

"I'm afraid that's beyond my skill level." He bent and kissed her forehead, then turned and left. I sat on the chair on the other side of her bed.

Daniel leaned forward. "Are you sure you can't tell me anything about your exciting job? You know I love your work stories."

Millicent grabbed the controls on her bed and pressed a button, lowering the backrest a bit, and settled into her pillow. "I'm too tired to talk about work, to be honest. How's Erin?"

"She's good. I finally bought her the new BMW she's been after me for. We picked it up the week before Christmas."

Millicent smiled. "You've been doing so well with the new job. Congratulations, and thanks for the generous gift." She shook her head and grabbed a small, red velvet box that was on the tray table hovering across the middle of her bed. And when I say hovering, I mean it was attached to a metal bar that led to wheels on the floor. With witches, hovering could mean so much more.

She opened the box and lifted out a delicate rose-gold necklace with a heart-shaped pendant. "Isn't it gorgeous, Lily?"

I leant closer. "It's stunning. Can you open it and put pictures inside?"

Millicent opened it, demonstrating the functionality. "I've always wanted something like this. I just never got around to buying one." She looked up at Daniel. "Thank Erin for me too. You're both so generous."

He grinned. "It's our pleasure. You should have nice things, Mill. You're awesome, and, as you know, you're my favourite cousin." He winked, and she laughed. How sweet that they were so close.

"Are you guys related on your mum or dad's side?"

Millicent put the necklace back in the box. "My mum is his dad's older sister. They also have an older brother, but he lives in Germany. His two kids are a bit younger. I think Elizabeth's doing her last year of high school, actually."

Daniel nodded. "Yep, and Elouise is in her first year of university. She's studying engineering. We're from a smart family. Geniuses, the lot of us." He laughed, so I figured he was kind of joking yet proud.

"Impressive," I said.

"I hear you and James are quite clever too, Lily. This baby is going to be an absolute genius, I bet, and a powerful you-know-what." I guessed he meant witch. I had to hand it to the guy; he was the proudest cousin I'd ever met.

"I bet this baby is going to be the best baby ever born." I grinned. "And it's our job to spoil it."

Millicent raised her brows. "*It?* Can't you say him or her?" She laughed.

"Soon we'll know what *it* is. Saying him or her is way too much work. You know I'm lazy at heart." She shook her head, bemusement on her face.

Daniel stood. "I guess I'd better get back to work. It was so nice to see you, Mill. I'll be back with Erin when the baby's born." He bent and kissed her cheek.

"Send her my love, and thanks again for the beautiful gift."

"Will do." He looked at me. "Lovely to meet you, Lily. I'm sure I'll see you again."

"I'm sure you will. Bye."

"Bye, ladies." He went into Millicent's private bathroom, and there was a tiny hum of magic—likely his doorway. I got up, went over, and knocked on the bathroom door. There was no answer, so I opened it. Yep. He was gone.

Being the lazy person I was, I sat in the chair Daniel had been in because it was closer to where I was. As I sat, James came in. "How are my three favourite people?" He walked around to the other side of the bed and sat on the chair.

Millicent rubbed her belly. "We're good."

"Shame you can't get three wishes when you do that." I laughed.

"Ha, if only!"

James grabbed Mill's hand. "Daniel's gone?"

"Yes. He said he'll come back with Erin to see the baby."

"It was nice of them to get you such an expensive present. His career's really taking off."

"It seems to be. He works so hard, and he did well at uni. He deserves it."

I didn't mean to change the subject and all the gushing over her cousin, but I needed information, as all good aunties did. "Well, I'm just glad you're okay. I've been so worried about you and the baby. Are you going to wait for it to happen naturally, or are they going to induce you? And if so, when?"

Millicent shrugged. "It's a wait and see. While my blood

pressure is being controlled with medication, we'll wait, but if the pre-eclampsia ramps up again, we'll induce. The baby's pointing in the right direction at least. *He or she* just doesn't want to come out yet."

James smiled a proud husband-father smile. "The baby is clearly too comfortable in there. And who could blame it?"

"James, *it*?!" Millicent mock scolded.

"Ha, it's not just me." I smirked.

Millicent raised a brow. "Lazy talking obviously runs in the family. I hope it isn't passed down to our little one."

James shifted his gaze from Millicent to over my shoulder. I turned. A nurse pattered in on soft-soled shoes. If it wasn't for James's reaction, I would've surely had a heart attack when she appeared next to me. What type of shoes did nurses wear? Was there a brand out there called Ninja Soles? I bet their company tagline would be "The soul of a ninja in each pair. Ensures silence, no matter the surface." It probably wasn't good for the patients though. I bet the nurses killed a few due to the heart attacks had when someone is just *there* and you didn't hear them coming. If I ran things, I'd make all nurses wear bells, like cats. Then there could be no sneaking, and, unlike clackety shoes, it would be a pleasant sound.

The nurse stood next to Millicent's bed. "I'm Abby, your nurse for this shift. How are you feeling today, Mrs Bianchi?"

"Tired, but otherwise okay, thanks."

"Great. I'm just going to take your blood pressure." She

turned to me. "Would you be able to move back for a minute?"

"Yes, sure." I stood and dragged my chair back so the nurse could get in next to Millicent's arm. She put the blood-pressure-machine cuff around her arm, turned the machine on, and waited while it buzzed and filled the cuff with air. After it worked out her blood pressure, the nurse did it one more time. Her poker face was almost as good as Angelica's. That was one thing I hated in hospital—you could never gauge what they were thinking, and, of course, I always thought the worst.

Abby wrote the results on Millicent's chart. "It's stable. I'll come back in a couple of hours." She smiled and left. I was about to ask about Millicent's cousin, but my phone rang.

Maybe Liv had gotten the funeral details, and I could start to plan when I'd make those interviews. I pulled my phone out of my pocket. Will's name was on the screen. *Please don't be bad news*. The sinking-fast sensation in my stomach was usually right, so I was pretty sure the universe was going to ignore my request. I answered the phone. "Hello, Will."

"Hi. You're not home."

"Um, no. How did you know?"

"Because I'm there. I came to get you."

"Get me for what?"

"There's been another suicide at Dover."

"Oh, crap. Okay, I'll be back in a minute. I'll just say goodbye to Mill and James."

"Say hello for me."

"Sure. Bye." My head fell back, and I stared at the ceiling. After letting out a tremendous sigh, I stood. "Sorry, guys, but I have to go. There's been another suicide at Dover."

James's brow furrowed. Millicent frowned and said, "Oh no. That's so sad."

"I know. Will's going to take me there to *help*."

James said the brotherliest thing he could, "Be careful, Lily."

"I will. Oh, and Will says hello to both of you. If anything happens with the baby, let me know." I bent and gave Millicent a quick hug. "See you later." I went to Millicent's bathroom, shut the door, and let my magic do the rest.

CHAPTER 6

Will held the large, black umbrella over my head. Sheeting rain angled towards my body and legs, but, thankfully, I was a witch, and I had a waterproof spell up. If any non-witches had been around, that would have been a no-no. Lucky for us, it seemed as if everyone else in the UK was sensible because no one else was out here braving the atrocious weather. A gull soared overhead, its baleful cry a portent of things to come.

My camera was pointed towards the cliff and the churning grey-green ocean beyond. "Show me the woman who jumped off the cliff this morning." There was no one standing there, but then a woman walked into frame. Crap. I fumbled with my camera and managed to flick it to video without missing too much.

She was thin, dressed in dark blue skinny jeans, black

knee-high boots, and a gorgeous red coat. The crimson coat was a bright beacon on a dreary day, radiant against the leaden ocean and sky. The woman stepped closer to the edge, then took one step back. She turned and seemed to look straight at me as if begging for help. Unlike the others I'd photographed, fear emanated from her blue eyes, so palpable it was like getting punched in the gut. I drew in a sharp breath and zoomed in on her young face—she couldn't have been more than early twenties.

A tear slid slowly down her face, stopping at her jaw, clinging desperately before being torn away by the wind. She turned back toward the sea. My heart raced.

"Nooooooo!" I started forward.

Will grabbed my arm as she stepped into the void.

I lowered the camera, dropped my head, and shut my eyes. The pressure of tears built behind my eyelids. Will worked his fingers under my chin and lifted my face gently. "What happened? Talk to me."

"It was in video. She didn't want to jump. I'm sure of it."

His Adam's apple bobbed as he swallowed. Concern shone from his eyes and each deep groove in his forehead, which just made me cry in earnest. He enfolded me in his arms and tucked my head under his chin.

Rain thrummed against the umbrella. The brine-laced air reeked of sorrow and tasted like tears. Will's voice was gentle. "Why don't we head home."

"Okay." I sniffed.

Will pulled away and looked down at me. "Are you okay?"

No. "Yes. I just need to process it." My magic always took its pound of flesh when I least expected it.

"Come here, then, and stay put." He gathered me in his arms again. The warm tingle of his magic caressed my nape. The sounds of spattering rain, keening wind, and the mournful cries of seagulls faded away. He whispered, "We're home."

"Thank you."

Will opened the reception-room door and took me to the living room. He lit the fire in the fireplace with a wisp of magic, and I sat in one of the armchairs. After Will had magicked us two coffees, he sat in the other armchair and held his free hand out. I knew what he was asking, so I passed him the camera.

As he watched the video, his jaw clenched. I didn't want to see the woman's haunted eyes again, so I turned my face away and stared into the fire. When he'd finished, he handed the camera back and shook his head. His voice subdued, he said, "No wonder you were upset. Your talent certainly creates confronting material. And being there, in real time…." He reached out and grabbed my hand. I squeezed it. At least I didn't have to go through this alone.

"Are you going to send it to Angelica now?"

"I think we can wait till she gets home. We'll show her then. Come here." He patted his lap. I sat and snuggled against his chest. He hugged me tight and kissed my forehead. "Love you, Lily. Thank you for helping us. I know it's not easy, but you're making an incredible difference to so many people. Never forget that."

"Thanks. I do know, but it's easy to forget when you're in the middle of watching someone suffer like that. She was so young." Grief spread over me, sinking into my skin, making me heavy, tired. She certainly hadn't looked like someone who wanted to die, and I'd been there too late. "Why can't we put up a magical barrier that stops people from jumping? We're witches. We could do it." The fact that the ability to save people existed but we weren't using it was criminal.

"We can't. Firstly, there is just too much distance to cover. If they don't jump from that exact spot, they'll walk further along till they find a spot. It would take an enormous amount of power to keep a barrier up 24/7. Secondly, we can't interfere. We need to stay under the radar, Lily. I'm sorry. It's frustrating for me too. That was one reason I joined the PIB—I wanted to help as much as I could."

"But doesn't it get frustrating having to solve a crime after the damage has been done? Wouldn't you prefer some of the crimes never happened?"

"Yes, but we can't save everyone from themselves. We can't go around making sure cars drive at safe speeds and steer properly, for instance. At least the non-witches are close to having that technology in lots of cars."

"Do witches ever nudge things like that along, with subtle suggestions, or magicking a solution, then guiding the non-witches to it?" That would be handy. "Couldn't we help that way?"

"Yes, but there are limitations—some things can only be achieved using magic indefinitely. We do what we can." He ran his hand down the back of my head a few times. I sighed, finally relaxing. "Oh, I've got the first funeral tomorrow, so you can probably call the day after to arrange an interview." And scrap that. No relaxation for me. My shoulders tensed, and I sat up to look at him.

"Thanks for the reminder. I was just getting comfortable. Now I'm all crabby again."

"Would you like to come to the funeral instead?" He raised a brow.

Oh, that was a low blow. "Okay, fine. Point made." Time to change the subject. I didn't want to talk about depressing things all night. "On Saturday, there's an art exhibition on in Westerham. Would you like to come with me? I'm going to ask Liv and Beren too."

His face relaxed. "Yep, that sounds good. What about we go somewhere nice for lunch afterwards?"

I smiled. "Sounds like a plan."

Other than Will showing Angelica the video when she got home, the rest of the evening was spent not talking about everything bad that was going on, but, unfortunately, it would be waiting for me tomorrow, and the day after that, and the day after that. And we were no closer to figuring this out than we were the day we saw Emily Armond, the first woman who jumped that we knew about. How many were there before her who might be connected to this, if it was, indeed, a crime and not the decision of someone who was depressed and thought this was the best choice?

Unfortunately, as the cliché said, only time would tell.

※

The next afternoon, after Emily's funeral, Imani, Liv, Ma'am, Will, and I gathered in the PIB conference room so Will could give us a rundown of what had happened. Sitting next to me, he leaned forward and put his forearms on the table, clasping his hands together. "There was a huge turnout. She must have been a popular woman. There were only two witches there; both were work colleagues, from what I overheard. Her children and grandchildren were there, even her ex-husband. I ended up at the wake afterwards. I managed to sneak in as waitstaff. I'm sorry, but I had to cast forget-in-motion spells on the real catering staff."

Huh? What the hell was that spell? Before I could ask, Ma'am folded her arms and served Will a harsh stare. "That's not ideal, Agent Blakesley. I didn't give you carte blanche to do whatever you saw fit. Please stay within the directives I give you next time."

The muscle in his jaw ticked, but he said, "Yes, Ma'am." Wow, the man had oodles of self-restraint. He would've had a good reason for doing what he did, and she would know that. Giving him a hard time wasn't very nice.

Because I had to know all the things, I asked, "What does the spell do, and why is it bad?"

Ma'am's curt tone made me wince. Poor Will. She was going all out in her disapproval. "You can explain, Agent Blakesley."

Will schooled his face to neutral and turned to me. "It's a spell that makes the person forget what they were going to say. I cast it specifically in relation to me. So, when a catering staff member approached me to ask who I was, they would get close, then wonder what they were going to say. I had to take my no-notice spell off so I wouldn't give anyone a heart attack serving drinks. I didn't want the two witches who were there wondering what I was doing trying to hide from everyone else. I stayed out of their line of sight at the grave, but it was going to be harder in a confined space."

"And why is it bad?"

"It tampers with the memory. They might have trouble remembering things for a few days, and if you're not careful, you can affect their memory for weeks to come." He stayed focussed on me, but his voice rose, probably as an annoyed reference to Ma'am. "But I was extremely careful, and it was necessary. Because I did that, I was able to listen in on many conversations." Now he did turn to Ma'am. "There was not one person there who thought she was depressed. She's never suffered from depression, and she was enjoying life. The only negative in her life, from what I could glean, was that her ex-husband was pestering her for money—apparently, he's in financial difficulty. She did give him twenty thousand pounds a year ago, but she'd said no to every other request. Listening to the ex's conversations, he wasn't angry at her or saying anything negative, and he's not a witch, so I don't know that it's worth chasing up that lead."

"So that's my angle, then," I said.

Ma'am looked at me as if I'd spoken elvish. And, no, elves didn't exist as far as I knew. But I'd read plenty of epic fantasies, and elves often had their own language. "When I interview her children and best friend. I imagine they'll be the best people to talk to. I'll say that often no one around the person realises they're depressed, and we're studying how to decipher subtle warning signs."

She gave a slow nod. "Ah, that makes sense, for a change." I opened my mouth to protest her insult, but she quickly turned to Will. "At the next funeral, I want you to be more careful. If you feel the need to cast any serious spells, call it in first for approval. Understood?"

"Yes, Ma'am." His voice was carefully neutral, which actually spoke volumes. There was not one person at this table who didn't know he was annoyed. And, I should note, the annoyance wasn't limited to Will. She'd just insulted me, then hurried onto something else as if it were nothing. Why did she always do that? I knew she cared about us, but sometimes, it was hidden under a mile of snark.

"Right, Olivia, I'd like you to research the woman who jumped last night. I've also decided to station an agent at the cliffs full-time. We'll have three shifts. Apart from the appalling number of deaths we can prevent, if there is magic involved, maybe we can get to the bottom of it quicker. It's not feasible for us to do this long term, but intercepting at least a few people should help."

"How will you stop them jumping?" I asked. "It's not

like you'll know who is going to jump and who isn't until they're actually leaping off the cliff."

"The agents will just have to start a conversation with anyone walking by themselves and do their best to glean what their intentions are."

The whole process still didn't make sense. "How are they going to explain the weird questions afterwards? I mean, how are you going to find out if a witch is involved and who it is without reading their minds, which is illegal?"

She sat back and rested her arms on the chair arms. "I'm going to give my agents special permission—as you know, it's our prerogative. It's warranted in this case. If the next three people who are there to commit suicide aren't affected by spells, we'll call off the watch. Now, dear, tomorrow you can call Emily's children and friend and make appointments to talk to them, then let Agent Jawara know."

"Yes, Ma'am." My stomach tensed. I was not looking forward to calling these people. There was no good way to bring up what I had to. What if they hung up on me?

"And you have the next funeral tomorrow; am I right, Will?"

"Yes, Ma'am. I'll report back to you tomorrow afternoon."

"Good. I think that's everything for today. We'll reconvene tomorrow afternoon for updates." Ma'am stood. "Thanks again, everyone." She made a doorway and left.

Imani and Will stood. "Come on, Will. We've got Operation Dolphin to attend to."

Huh? "Operation Dolphin? Are there witch dolphins? I didn't think witches could shift."

Imani looked at me like my IQ had just dropped fifty points. "There are no such things as shifters, Lily. It's just a made-up code name."

My cheeks burned. Lily the Idiot strikes again. But to be fair, she believed in ghosts, and need I say it again, but *witches*. "Oh, right."

Will chuckled. "Never change." He bent and kissed the top of my head. "I'll see you tonight, around seven."

At least I had something to look forward to later. I held onto that thought for the rest of the day.

CHAPTER 7

Cynthia and I sat opposite each other in a café in Sevenoaks. Otto's Coffee House & Kitchen was in a quaint white building. The warm interior featured timber floorboards, white walls, dark timber ceiling, and a large fireplace. Even though the building was old and retained original features, the décor suggested clean modernity.

I'd wanted to get this over and done with as quickly as possible, but Emily's best friend, Cynthia, had wanted to meet for brunch. As sad as this was, the food on the plate in front of me looked amazing. Sourdough toast covered with smashed avocado, poached egg, rocket lettuce, and bacon. And before anyone called me a carelessly spending Millennial, the prices weren't too bad, and it was healthy. What was everyone's fixation with smashed avocado being the thing that ruined young peoples' futures?

My phone was on the table, face up, and I was recording the conversation with Cynthia's permission. She sipped her tea, then carefully placed the cup on the saucer. Eyes red from crying, the blue in her irises stood out. She shook her head. "I just can't understand it. She was happy, at least she said she was. We were even planning a holiday to Australia."

"Was she having any problems with anyone she cared about?"

"Her ex was begging her for money every five minutes, but she found him irritating rather than upsetting. She had been dating someone for a few months, but they broke up before Christmas."

That seemed pretty significant. "That could've been a trigger."

She stared at the scones on her plate. "Maybe, but she was the one who broke it off."

"Did she ever self-medicate with drugs, food, or alcohol?"

She looked up at me, her brow lined with what could've been frustration. "No. There was nothing to medicate. She enjoyed a glass of wine, like the rest of us, but never drugs, and she was slim, so that would be a 'no' to the food as well. She indulged every now and then, but she lived a healthy life."

"How often did she interact with people? Isolation can sometimes be a factor."

"Even though she was retired, she went to yoga, had her hair done every week, went for facials, and we caught up once a week too. I know she spoke to her children at least every second day. They're both busy with their own families, of course, but they were still close."

We'd been here for thirty minutes, and I was running out of questions, yet there was nothing to suggest she'd been depressed or that anyone hated her. "So there was no one she was fighting with?"

"No." She finished her tea and looked at her watch. "Look, this is hard for me. I don't want to think about all these negatives, and I have an appointment to get to. Emily was a happy, vibrant woman, and I just don't know what happened. If witnesses on the day hadn't seen it with their own eyes, I would've said someone pushed her. It must have been an accident. Maybe she didn't mean to step so close? I wish you well with your research, and I hope it ends up helping people, but I have nothing else to add. Sorry." She stood.

"Okay. Thanks for your time, and I've got the bill. I appreciate you meeting with me today, and, again, I'm sorry you've lost your friend."

She nodded and left. I'd only half eaten my meal, but even though it was delicious, I'd lost my appetite. It seemed that interview was all for nothing. I'd made her talk about someone she'd just lost, and it hadn't helped either of us. My stomach gurgled in protest as a maelstrom of nausea assailed it. How was I supposed to do this over and over again? Emily's two children had refused to speak to me, but Angelica wanted me to talk to the ex-husband. Hmm, there was something small. Maybe her most-recent ex had done something? We should find out who he is. Had he gone to the funeral? If he had, at least Will would know who it was. If I could interview him, maybe it would provide a clue. He might even be a witch. That would be very interesting. Of course, Cynthia had left, and now I wished I'd asked for his name, but she might have found that weird since her friend had supposedly broken up with him ages ago. What could he have possibly added to my enquiries that her best friend couldn't? Cynthia might have become suspicious of what I was doing.

I paid and left. The building was on a corner. I walked along the side street and met Imani, who was sitting in her car, waiting. At least it wasn't raining. That was another thing to be thankful for. Why was it getting harder and harder to find the positives? Was my life that terrible?

I hopped into the car and put my seat belt on. Imani looked at me. "How'd you go? Get anything useful?"

"I don't think so. You may as well listen to it as we drive, and then you can tell me." I pressed Play on the recording, and as she drove us home, I relived fifteen of the last thirty minutes of my life with a grieving stranger. Not one of my finest moments. I stared out the window in a futile attempt at distracting myself.

When we reached Angelica's, we went into the living room, sat on one of the Chesterfields, and finished listening to it. When it was done, Imani looked at me, her poker face activated. "Okay, so you're right: there wasn't much in that to go on." This was one time I wished she didn't agree with me.

"I was thinking that maybe I should interview the ex-boyfriend, or at least find out if he's a witch first. What do you think?"

"Interviewing him might be jumping the gun, but I think we do need to find out who he is and if he's a witch. I'll text Liv and ask her to find out." Imani pulled out her phone and got to work.

"Oh, are you working tomorrow? There's a photographic exhibition on at the local gallery. Will, B, and Liv are coming. We're going to grab lunch somewhere afterwards. Wanna join us?"

She put her phone back in her pocket. "Sounds great. I'm on call tomorrow, so if anything comes up, I'll have to run, but, at this stage, it looks okay."

"Yay! It'll be nice to just relax for a change." My phone rang, as if the very mention of the word "relax" was an invitation to stir things up. The universe was always listening, damn it. Oh my God, it was James. *Please be good news.* "Hello, James. What's up?"

James sounded worried and slightly dazed. "Hey, Lily. Just letting you know that the drugs aren't working anymore, and they've decided to induce. This will probably take a few hours, but all going well, we'll have a baby by tonight."

Eek, exciting yet worrying. Millicent wasn't okay yet, and neither was the baby, but surely they dealt with this kind of thing often, and it would all be fine. "Do you want me to come to the hospital for moral support?"

"Um, no. Mill and I have this for now, but thanks. I'll let you know when you have a niece or nephew."

I grinned—it was impossible not to. Excited flutters took

up residence in my chest. "Okay. I'll be waiting for your call. Love you, and good luck."

"Love you too. Bye."

Imani was staring at me, an expectant look on her face. "Tell me. Tell me."

"They're inducing Millicent now. We should have a Millicent-James version 2.0 by tonight. Oh my God, this is so exciting. I can't wait. I just hope everything goes well."

Imani grinned. "It really is. Let me know when you know. I love babies. I can't wait to meet him or her."

"Will do. So, now what?"

"It's time for me to go back to work. I'll just send your recording to my phone." Her magic tingled my scalp, and she said, "Today's recording on Lily's phone will be sent to mine in one second's time." I sighed. She was so much better at rhyming than I was. "Okay, I'm off. And don't forget to let me know about the baby."

"I won't. Promise." She gave me a quick hug, then disappeared.

Alone again.

Funny how that bothered me. I used to love being by myself. Not that I hated alone time, but it wasn't as if I could just go wherever I wanted without an escort like I could back in Sydney. Wandering around by myself taking photos or going for a run or a surf was not doable, which meant most of my alone time was being stuck inside. No wonder it bothered me. I'd be beyond happy when we shut the snake group down, and I could get my life back. Hopefully catching them also meant solving the mystery of what happened to my parents.

Restlessness was setting in. I stood and went to the window. At least the sky was blue today, but it was still cold. It would have been awesome to go for a run, but since I couldn't do that by myself, it wasn't going to happen. I did need to exercise though. I magicked my laptop to myself and magicked my clothes into T-shirt and black tights. I found a Pilates workout video on YouTube and got to it. Didn't matter what happened, I would not lose my positive attitude, and exercise always helped me maintain it.

It was time to sweat.

After working out, I showered and sat on my bed to read. I must have dozed off, sloth that I was, because I awoke to my phone ringing and a dark room. I wiped the drool from the corner of my mouth and fumbled for my phone. I was still half asleep, so by the time I found it tangled in my covers, it had stopped ringing. Thank goodness for the "missed calls" feature.

James.

I sat up and called him back. "Sorry, I missed your call. Has she had the baby?"

"Yes. It's a girl! She's so beautiful, Lily. And Mill is doing well too, although she's exhausted. We'd love for you to come see her."

"Congratulations! Oh my God, I'm an auntie! Oh,

Imani wanted me to tell her when the baby came. Is it okay if she visits too?"

The smile in his voice was unmistakable. "Yes, of course. When Millicent's had enough, she'll let you know. Her parents are here at the moment, but it's fine if you come."

"Let me just wash the drool off my face, and I'll be there."

"What?"

I laughed. "I had an unscheduled nap, which is why I missed your call. See you soon!" I ran to the bathroom, magicked a change of clothes, grabbed my Nikon—because I was totally going to take some professional shots of them on such an incredible day—and made my doorway to the hospital. Once I was there, I texted Imani the details. And thankfully, this time there was no one in the cubicle. Phew!

I dropped into the gift shop on the way to Mill's room and picked up a huge bunch of flowers. I couldn't believe I was about to meet a new little person who was actually related to me. It was about time our family grew. I blinked back tears. Mum and Dad would've been overjoyed, but they'd never get to meet James's new baby. The magma of anger that silently flowed through my core bubbled to the surface. Whoever had robbed our family of every special moment and every quiet, loving word and hug would be lucky if they survived my wrath. *I'm coming for you, and I'm leaving mercy behind.* I shuddered at my own vehemence. Once my volcano erupted, it would obliterate everyone in its way.

Maybe even me.

I stopped just outside Millicent's room and took some

calming breaths. The last thing I wanted to do was allow those evil pigs to encroach on such a happy event. I pushed all the negativity out of my mind and went in.

James was on the other side of the bed, and Millicent's parents were on this side, their backs to me, blocking my view of Millicent and the baby. I assumed she was holding the baby since I couldn't see it anywhere. *Hmm, not* it, *Lily,* her. The sooner they told me her name, the better. I smiled. I had a niece.

James looked up and grinned at me.

"Hi," I said, moving to the foot of the bed. Millicent's parents turned towards me, and Millicent looked up from the swaddled bundle in her arms. "How are you?"

"Tired and incredibly happy." Her smile was that of someone exhausted but content. "Lily, these are my parents, Robert and Anne. This is James's sister."

They both smiled, and Anne said, "Lovely to meet you. I was wondering when we'd finally get an introduction." Her blonde hair was cut in a similar shoulder-length bob to Millicent, and she was petite of frame, just like my sister-in-law. Considering how nice Mill was, I had to assume her parents were too.

"Lovely to meet you too." I smiled and turned to Millicent. "Let's get some photos of you and the baby, and then you, James, and the baby." I held up my camera and shut off my magic. Bereft at its absence, it was an effort to maintain my smile. It took a moment, but I got myself together.

I took a few shots of Millicent holding the most adorable baby I'd ever seen. I wasn't really a baby person, but, in an instant, my niece changed that for me. I asked Millicent to place her in her little plastic hospital crib, which she did, and I took a few close-ups of her sweet face and tiny hands. Millicent then gathered her up again. James sat on the bed next to Millicent, put his arm around her, and looked at the camera. I took a few shots like that, then of the parents gazing lovingly upon their daughter. I finished and looked at Millicent's parents. "Would you like some with Millicent as well?"

Her mother put her hand to her chest. "Oh, would you? That would be lovely. Thank you!" Robert and Anne moved into shot, and I did my thing.

I lowered my camera. "I'm done. Um… would I be able to hold her?"

Millicent's eyes lit up with her grin. "Of course." She handed the baby to James, who brought her around to my side of the bed.

"Sit there, Lily, and you can hold her." I did as asked, and James placed the tiny, warm bundle into my waiting arms.

I stared down at the precious sleeping babe. Her chubby-cheeked pink face was relaxed and sweet in sleep. She had a button nose and lots of dark hair. My heart swelled to twice its normal size, and I thought it might burst from overwhelming love. I whispered, "She's perfect." I wanted to plant thousands of kisses on her face, but I was sure no one would appreciate it if I woke her. I guessed I'd have time for all that later. I looked up at James, tears moistening my eyes. We smiled at each other but needed no words. We were sharing the bittersweet joy of having this incredible human in our lives without our parents.

I swallowed and gazed back down at the baby. My voice cracked when I spoke. "Your grandparents on daddy's side would have loved to meet you, sweetness. I'm sorry you won't get to know them, but I'll fill you in on how awesome they were one day. Know that you're loved. I'm Auntie Lily, by the way, and when Mummy and Daddy are being mean and telling you that you can't have another piece of cake, you just come and visit me, and we'll eat all the cake you want, and play all the games. Love you, precious." This time, I couldn't resist. I carefully bent my head and placed the gentlest kiss on her forehead.

James had been hovering the whole time, and I could tell he was itching to have his daughter back. I grinned. "Okay, Daddy, here you go." He smiled and bent to take her as I gingerly lifted the baby and placed her into his arms. "Has she got a name yet?"

Millicent shook her head. "No. We have three on the shortlist. We're giving ourselves another day to decide."

James made his way back to Millicent. As he placed the baby in her arms, the baby let out a tiny grumble, which quickly turned into a halting cry. Mill's mother laughed. "Someone's hungry. We'll go and grab a cup of tea and leave you to it, won't we, Robert?"

"Yes, love." Millicent's father smiled down at her. "We'll be back soon."

I stood. "I've got a few things to do at home, so I'll pop away too, let you settle into your new reality." I grinned.

"Congratulations, you two. You've made the cutest baby on the planet." I gave Millicent a kiss on the cheek, then went and gave my brother the biggest hug ever. "Call me if you need anything."

James smiled. "Will do."

"Oh, Imani should be coming at some point. I thought she'd be here soon after me, but she must've been held up at work."

"Not a problem. Bye, Lily."

"See you later, alligator." I made my way to Millicent's bathroom. What a day. Elation and melancholy danced a timeless, heart-wrenching waltz inside me. But that was life, and we'd all do our best to get through it for as long as we could.

Except for those who had jumped recently.

Pushing that thought from my mind and filling it with the joy of my new niece, I made my doorway and went through.

CHAPTER 8

The next morning, I was still on a baby high. I texted James to make sure everyone was still doing well, and then I got ready for a, hopefully, good day. The fact that it wasn't raining and the top temp would be ten degrees was positive too. Beren and Imani had met Will, Liv, and me at Angelica's; then we walked to the gallery.

When we reached our destination, I paused, took a deep breath, then opened the art-gallery door. Behind me, Will put his hands on my waist in support. It was weird coming back. The last time I was here, I was investigating the disappearance of my art teacher. I'd had to date the gallery owner's son to find out what had happened. Sadly, he'd killed her, and her gorgeous fox. Since then, new owners had bought the business and renamed it London Gallery—after the street it was on rather than the city.

The layout was unchanged—three large rooms—but the timber floor had been stained almost black, and the walls were stark white. The first room contained black-and-white images, and the second two rooms featured colour photographs, all of them portraits or African nature studies. So many stunning images, from giraffes and lions to elderly people with deep-set wrinkles that told a thousand stories. From my friends' comments, they were impressed too.

We stopped in front of a colour shot of a black panther lying relaxed on a large fallen tree trunk, its tail slunk over the edge, hugging the curve of the log, the tail tip touching the earth. The panther's majestic green eyes stared straight into the camera, its shiny black coat impressively regal. If the lion was the king of the jungle, the panther was the prince of darkness. If only I could have one as a pet. It had to be the most gorgeous type of cat there was.

"You like this one?" Will asked.

"Love would be more the word I'd use."

"Why don't you buy it? I'm sure Angelica wouldn't mind you putting it up somewhere."

I laughed. "Um, it's three thousand pounds. I'm saving for my own place. I'll never be able to afford something over here if I keep spending my money."

"When was the last time you spent money?" Liv asked.

"Um… ages ago, I suppose, but, still, I can't justify spending that much on something that won't be useful. Once I have my own place sorted, I'll save for artwork. They're worth it, but it's just not the right time for me." I could sell my apartment in Sydney and buy something here, but I'd still need to add to the funds, and I wasn't quite ready to let my Australian home go just yet. And as much as I loved that photograph, I couldn't justify spending that much on it, especially since I didn't have a steady income. It felt like a want rather than a need—okay, it actually wasn't a need at all.

"Hmm."

I turned and looked at Will. "What does 'hmm' mean?"

He shrugged. "Nothing, just hmm."

I raised my brow, not convinced, but I had no idea what he was going for with the hmm. Was it a criticism of my unwillingness to be frivolous, or did he not want me to get my own place? Gah, who knew? And it didn't matter.

We moved on and finally reached the last picture. Beren put his hands in his jeans pockets. "I don't know about you lot, but I'm starving. Let's go grab some lunch."

"Sounds good to me. I'm super hungry." Liv linked her arm through mine, and we wandered back through the gallery, to the front door, Imani, Will, and Beren behind. Liv opened the gallery door, and Will's phone rang.

He looked at his phone. "I have to take this. Go on, and I'll catch up."

Beren nodded and nudged Liv and I out onto the street, Imani behind him. I resisted the urge to pout. "I hope that's not work calling him in. We hardly ever get to do fun things together."

Beren walked next to me along the footpath. "It's just part of the job, but I'm sure that whatever it is, he'll be able to have lunch with us."

I sighed. "I sure hope so."

We reached a T intersection, Westerham Hall diagonally opposite us. Imani peered across at the car park, which was full of cars and people. There were even kids with helium balloons. "What's happening there today? Do they have markets or something? I love a good market."

I remembered browsing the internet for local events. "It's some promo thing for a local plastic surgeon."

Footsteps sounded behind us. I turned. Will grinned, his dimples super cute. How did I get so lucky? "You guys haven't gone far. What's happening?"

Beren affected a serious expression. "We're considering whether or not to check out the plastic surgery fun day."

I nodded. "Yes, because nothing says 'party time' like getting a nose job." I ran my finger down my nose. Nope, all good here, thanks. "Although, maybe they have snacks. They could feed us lots of treats, then suck the fat back out."

"Loves, we're missing out. I want to see what kind of crowd something like this attracts. I feel that a trip across the road is in order. A short detour, if you will." Imani rubbed her hands together.

I gave her a side-eyed glance. "You're a weirdo. You that, right?"

She waggled her brows. "You know it, lovie. Enough talk. Let's go." She looked both ways and crossed to the Westerham Hall car park. We, being the loyal friends we were, followed. If one of us was going to be silly, it didn't hurt for the rest of us to support them.

Once we reached the other side, Will slipped his arm around my waist. "Just FYI, if you get anything sucked out, I'm going to get lip filler and bum implants." His lip twitched as he tried to keep a straight face, and Liv snickered.

I gave him my most serious face. "You're only allowed to get bum implants if you can dance like Beyoncé. You get it, you gotta shake it. Besides, you need pec and bicep implants way more." I took that opportunity to unashamedly feel his pecs, which were actually quite firm and totally perfect. Nobody could blame me, surely?

"Ooh, burned, my scrawny friend." Beren laughed.

"I think you mean brawny." Will lifted his arm and flexed his bicep, even though we couldn't see it through his black turtleneck jumper.

We reached the hall door. The A-frame out the front said, "Get your free consultation today! If you want perfection in your reflection, Dr Ezekal can help."

I raised a brow. "*Perfection in your reflection*? There's no such thing, and besides, it's subjective." So many people were sad they weren't perfect, but why couldn't they just be happy? There was more to this world than looking like the latest fad. I folded my arms, and a woman came out the door. My mouth wanted to fall open, but I didn't let it. Her nose came to the smallest point, so much so that it was hardly there, and her lips were humungous. So huge that if they were removable, you could use them to make balloon animals at a kid's party. And how did she even breathe through those pin-hole nostrils? After she'd passed, I said, "I rest my case."

Imani smirked. "She probably thinks she looks gorgeous. At least she's happy. And not all plastic surgery looks so obvious. I bet you've seen people who've had it, and you didn't even notice."

"True, I suppose, and I'm all for people being happy with themselves. But at what cost do aesthetics come at?" I wasn't convinced. "I mean, I know some people need it for reconstructive reasons, but surgery is so risky. You could get infections afterwards or die from the anaesthetic. The whole thing scares me." I shuddered. "Just before I came here, a woman in Sydney had half her face eaten off by an infection, and another one died when her beautician injected her with something she shouldn't have. Besides, what's wrong with normal lips? Seriously, they're lips. They all look fine the way they are. Next thing you know, people will be wanting fat earlobes."

Liv laughed. "I think that's about the only body part they don't currently operate on, although I'm sure someone somewhere has probably had their lobes plumped up."

"I don't know," Will said, a sultry look on his face. "Ears really do it for me. The plumper, the better."

"I'll start saving," I said as I pulled the door to the hall open. Massive pictures of perfect faces and bodies had been put up around the place. It was as if we were visiting another exhibition.

A woman in her thirties stood just inside the entry. Her blonde hair was tied back in a neat bun, and blue eyes gazed out of her slim face. She smiled in greeting. Her teeth formed two perfectly white and straight rows that were like a flash of neon in her heavily made-up face. "Welcome to our open day. How can I help you?"

I smiled. "Hi. We just wanted to come in and have a look."

"I'm sorry, but this open day is for serious clients only. Dr Ezekal doesn't have time to consult with tyre kickers."

"How do you know I don't want plastic surgery?" Okay, I totally didn't want it, but still, if there were hor d'oeuvres on offer, I could consider it for five minutes.

"Your body language, and, if I looked like you, I wouldn't do anything. We only work with patients we feel really need the surgery. I'm sorry."

I folded my arms, wondering what her angle was. "So you're saying I'm already perfect?"

She looked at me for a beat too long. "Ah, yes, that's exactly what I'm saying. It was lovely to meet you, but I'm going to have to ask you and your perfect friends to leave."

I looked at Will. He gave a small shrug. I supposed today was going well until this, and the woman was right that we were just tyre kickers. There was no point in causing trouble. "Okay. Bye."

We all filed outside. "That was weird," said Liv. "You'd think they'd want as many clients as possible."

"Could be, they're actually ethical," said Beren. "It's not unheard of, you know."

Time to look at the positive side. "True. Well, nice to

know they're doing a good job." My stomach grumbled loud enough for everyone to hear, and everyone laughed.

Imani looked at my stomach. "Time to feed the beast?"

"You know it."

We walked back to Westerham's main street and turned right into Market Square. Our destination—the Rendezvous Brasserie—was a two-storey white and dark blue-grey building with one third-floor dormer window, only a few doors down from Napoli E, the Italian restaurant I'd been to a few times. I'd never eaten at the Rendezvous, but Imani swore it was the best French food around.

Beren opened the door for us and came in last. The interior had light-coloured timber floors and white and beige walls. It was hard not to close my eyes as I savoured the delicious garlic and roasting-meat scents coming from the kitchen. A few tables were already occupied, but it looked as if we'd just beaten the weekend lunch rush.

A waitress approached us. "Can I help you?"

I'd actually booked the table, so I stepped forward. "We've got a booking for 1:00 p.m. for five people under the name of Bianchi."

"Righto, let me have a look." She went to her reservations book, then returned with a radiant smile. "This way please." She led us to a table by the window, and we sat.

While we perused the menu and decided on food, two young women sat at the table next to us. One was tall and slim, her long dark hair straight and shiny; the other was short and skinny, but—well, there was no subtle way to say it —her boobs were huge and way too big for her frame. They just couldn't be real. And I didn't want to stare, but were they uneven? Maybe she'd gone to the plastic-surgery open day to see about getting them evened up. Hopefully she didn't want to go bigger. I hated to think how sore her back was, plus goodbye to sleeping on your stomach.

"Lily?" Will leaned over and waved his hand in front of my face. "What do you want?"

"Huh?"

"To eat." He rolled his eyes and turned to the waitress, who was patiently standing there, electronic ordering device in hand.

"Oh, sorry." My cheeks burned. Seemed as if I couldn't go two days without embarrassing myself. "Um…." I looked down at the menu again. "I'll have the pan-roast duck breast, thanks." I resisted the urge to quack, and then I felt bad. Those poor cute ducks. I was going to eat one. But did I feel bad enough to change my order? Hypocrite that I was, the answer was no. Bad Lily.

Liv ordered wine for the table, and Will poured me a glass of water—he knew I didn't like wine that much. Plus, since I'd been a target for bad witches, I wanted to be alert at all times. I hadn't worked out how to sleep with one eye open yet, but I was working on it.

Imani started talking about my new niece, but before she could get too far into the story, cackling came from the two women at the next table. The tall, modelish one had her back to me, but her cockney-accented voice reached me just fine. "But they look good!"

The other one had a similar accent, but I had to strain

to hear her. "I'm just 'avin' trouble findin' a bra that fits both of 'em. It's weird, right? They look the same, but they aren't."

"But they are the same. I mean, well, no one's are exactly the same, but there's no way I can tell them apart."

Imani was staring at me as if to say, what the actual hell? I giggled. It was probably time to stop eavesdropping, not that the loud one made that easy. We finally managed to get our conversation back on track, and before I knew it, it was time to leave. We were going back to Angelica's for everyone to travel from there.

On our return walk, Will's phone rang. Was it too much to ask for a PIB-free day? "Hello, Ma'am. Yes?" He frowned and listened. "Okay. No, not a problem. Yes. Bye."

Liv unlocked the front door, and Will turned to me. "I'm sorry, but can you take another trip to Dover with me?"

Damn. Well, half a great day was better than none, right? "Yeah, sure." As I magicked my camera to myself, shards of dread sliced my insides. I hated lying, but sometimes it was necessary. "Okay. I'm ready." Stepping through my doorway, I was anything but.

CHAPTER 9

I was living my best life… *not*. Saturday afternoon, and I was sitting at the PIB conference-room table with Imani, Will, Ma'am, Olivia, and Agent Johanssen, the blond, gorgeous six-foot-five Norse-god-looking agent who'd been on duty at the cliffs when the latest poor soul jumped. The jumper was a young lady who'd been a friend of the last victim, who I now learned was Ellie Fisher. Her gorgeous yet terrified face had haunted my sleeping hours since I'd videoed her last living moments.

Ma'am was grilling poor Agent Johanssen. As sorry as I felt for him, we needed to know what had happened. "What time did you first see the woman who jumped, Ingrid Braun, I believe her name is?"

"At approximately 1:00 p.m."

"Was she by herself?"

"Yes, Ma'am, but there were others walking and

enjoying the view." Who would've thought someone would jump in the middle of the day, in front of other people? But come to think of it, I'd known someone back in Sydney who was waiting at the train station when someone jumped in front of a train, in front of a packed platform. I guessed when you're in the midst of despair, nothing but your objective matters. So much pain in the world. The heaviness of it settled uncomfortably into my chest.

Ma'am had a somewhat gentle version of her poker face on—it suggested scant emotion in the form of calmness and understanding. She must be trying to make this as easy as possible. "Did you have any warning she would jump when you first saw her?"

He shook his head. "No, Ma'am."

"At what point did you realise she was going to do it?"

He looked at the tabletop for a moment before meeting his boss's gaze. "When she was near the edge of the cliff. Four others were close to the edge, so I was within six feet of them. I wasn't sure if any of them would jump, but the group near her seemed happy and were taking photos, enjoying the view. The young woman, however, appeared focussed, even stressed. She looked across at me just before she jumped. That's when I knew. I cast a hold spell, but it was repelled, and I froze for a minute. By the time I could move again, she'd jumped." Agent Johanssen also had his poker face on, but the telltale tic in his jaw muscle gave insight into his feelings.

Wow, that was tough and unexpected. "Excuse me, Ma'am," I said.

"Yes, dear?"

"Was Ingrid a witch?" If she was, that would make her our first witch suicide in this case.

"No, Lily, she wasn't."

"So how come the spell bounced back? Did someone put a return to sender on her?" This was a massive clue. No matter how the spell had returned to Agent Johanssen, a witch was definitely involved.

Ma'am gave the Norse-god agent a probing look. "You *did* check her with your other-sight, did you not?"

He sat up straighter. "Of course I did. She wasn't a witch, and there were no spells showing in her aura. It was likely a side effect of whatever spell she was under."

Ma'am scrutinised him a moment longer before answering. "Right. So, other than this small piece of information, us guarding the cliffs was a colossal waste of time. Which leaves me to wonder, where to from here?" It quickly became apparent that she wasn't going to answer her own question. She stared at us one by one, waiting for input.

Imani braved the possibility of incurring Ma'am's wrath. "I think it would be prudent to ascertain what commonality the two friends had. Who were they dealing with that would want them both dead? And why? Friends tend to do the same things as each other, so maybe it would be easier to find a link by interviewing both families or friends, as they would have shared at least some of the same friends. Interviewing connections of the other victims could mean wading through a lot of useless information, especially if one of them isn't actually involved in this case. It could throw us off. But two friends within one day of each other is too coincidental, especially with magic being confirmed in the second case."

Will nodded. "I think we should get involved as law enforcement. We can say we're looking into this because the two were known to each other, and we're making sure there's been no foul play. We should be sure to stress that it's just a formality."

A pen appeared in Ma'am's hand, and she tapped it on the table while she considered the proposals. She finally stopped tapping. "Right. I'm going to send you and Agent Jawara, Agent Blakesley. Due to the number of interviews you're going to conduct, I imagine this will take at least a week, but I'd like you to get through them as quickly as possible. It would be preferable if we could wrap them up in a few days. I'd put James and Beren on this too, but James is on parental leave for two weeks, and I'd rather not send Beren by himself." She pressed her lips together briefly, a small gesture for a normal person, but a massive tell from her—she wasn't happy. "We've got so many cases going, and we need to train more agents, but they're not giving me the budget. It's beyond frustrating." She huffed. "Anyway, that's not your problem. Everyone is dismissed but Agent Johanssen. I have another assignment for you now that we've seen our presence on the clifftop is redundant."

"Yes, Ma'am."

Everyone else stood, and we exited via the normal door. Will, ever the gentleman, was the last one out, so he shut the door. "Sorry we had to cut our day short, Lily."

"I know. Me too. But solving this case is important. Each day sees another person dead. It's horrible." My shoulders sagged. "I'll see you when I see you."

He put his finger under my chin and tipped my head back so I was looking into his dreamy blue eyes. "I'll be home for dinner." He dropped his hand without giving me a kiss—we were at work, and it wasn't appropriate. Stupid work.

"Okay. I'll see you then." I gave him a small wave, and he and Imani walked off in the direction of his office.

Liv linked her arm in mine. "Beren and I are still free. Maybe we could have a game of Monopoly or something."

Oh, joy. I was notoriously bad at board games. "Okay. I can deal with it as long as it isn't Trivial Pursuit. I have zero general knowledge."

She laughed. "I'm awesome at it. If you ever have to play, just team up with me. I've got your back."

I grinned. "It's a deal. Actually, have you guys seen the baby yet?"

"No. Beren worked late last night, and by the time we could have gone, it was too late."

"We could go visit Mill and the baby." I grinned as my heart swelled with happiness.

"That's an awesome idea. Let's grab Beren and go."

"Yes, let's." I made our doorway, and off we went.

CHAPTER 10

Sunday. Here it was, but Will was at work. At least I got to sleep in. I dressed and trudged downstairs to find Olivia. Voices came from the living room, so I went there before the kitchen. Liv and Beren were sitting in the armchairs drinking tea in front of the fireplace. "Good morning."

They turned. "Morning, Lily," Liv said.

Beren smiled. "Hey, sleepyhead. We were going to wait for you, then go to Costa, but we gave up. It's almost lunchtime."

"What time is it?" I asked because I'd left my phone upstairs. I really should get a watch. Hmm, maybe one of those Apple ones. I could pair them with Airpods for when I ran. That was something to think about.

Beren looked at his phone. "Ten thirty."

I rolled my eyes. "Mr Exaggerator. It's not that late after

all, especially for a Sunday. In fact, I think I'm up too early. I should go back to bed."

Liv put her teacup on the small table next to her chair. "Ha ha, very funny. If you want, we can go to Costa now. We had breakfast two hours ago, and I'm getting a bit peckish for a croissant." She turned to Beren. "What say you, oh, witchy one?"

"I say, sounds good to me." He stood, teacup in hand, grabbed her cup, and magicked them both away, hopefully to the dishwasher.

I gazed out the window. "Another cold but not-raining day. Perfect weather for walking." A squirrel scampered up the tree. Oh my God, they were so damn cute. I'd never get sick of seeing the little furry creatures zip about. Seeing squirrels was usually the highlight of my day.

Olivia followed my line of sight and laughed. "No wonder you have that goofy look on your face." She turned to Beren, and they both said at the same time, "Squirrels!"

"You betcha! I think they were invented just to cheer people up. How could you not feel happy while watching squirrels?"

Liv smirked. "It is possible, believe it or not."

"I choose not." I grinned. "So, are we going to get this double-chocolate-muffin-and-cappuccino show on the road?"

"Lead the way," said Beren. So I did.

As usual, the first step into Costa was an olfactory delight. It was as if I was engulfed in a deliciously soft cloud of chocolate and coffee. *Oh, what would I do without you, sweet, sweet Costa?*

"Lily." Liv giggled.

"What?"

"Did you just moan?"

I bit my lip. "Um… I don't think so, but it's entirely possible."

Beren grinned. "You definitely moaned. Lucky Will wasn't here to see it—he'd likely get jealous."

I grinned back. "He gets it. He knows he has to share me with Costa."

Liv shook her head. "That sounds all kinds of wrong."

We lined up, ordered, and found a table in the middle of the chattering throng common on a Sunday. Liv and Beren sat opposite me. My phone dinged with a message. I pulled it out. James.

Hey, Lily, if you want to see the baby later, we'll be at home. Just getting discharged now.

Hey, bro. Sounds good. Is it okay if Beren and Liv come?

Yep. Just let them know that if the baby is asleep, I'm not waking her up. Also, if she's asleep, it's likely Mill will be too. Maybe text me just before you leave.

Not a problem. Xx

Before I could give the news to my friends, an argument at the table behind me caught my attention. Being the busybody I was, I strained to listen. A woman said, "You need to slow down—at least cut back to two or three days a week."

An older man's irritated response was in a posh accent. "No. Cutting back my hours will lead to retirement, and

I'm not ready. I love my work. You know that. If you want to cut down your days, I understand. You do so much for me."

A loud sigh. "That's not why I'm asking you. You know why we're having this conversation. You're so tired at the end of the day. I worry you'll get sick. How many seventy-year-olds do you know who work the hours you do? It's not healthy, Dad."

Liv looked at me and was about to say something, but I put my finger in front of my lips, jerked my head backwards, then pointed at my ear. I needed to know how this was going to play out.

The old man laughed. "Don't worry, darling. I'm feeling pretty good for an old fellow. I promise I'll cut my hours, but not for another couple of years. What was the point of having our promotional day yesterday for me to just cancel all those new surgeries we'll get from it? I want to make sure you're taken care of when I die."

"You know it's not about the money. We have plenty of it." She sounded tired, frustrated.

"I'll admit, I love my work. It's so rewarding, helping people. Please don't ask me to give it up."

The woman heavy sighed, her tone resigned when she said, "Okay, Dad, but we'll have this conversation again in a few months. Okay?"

"Okay." They were quiet after that, and our food and drinks arrived.

I carefully consumed the froth and chocolate at the top of my cappuccino before taking a sip. Olivia was looking at me with an expression I knew well. I lowered my voice. "I wanted to listen. Is it a crime?"

"No, but it's not polite. And now I feel bad because I listened too. It's all your fault."

"They don't even know we heard, and, besides, if they don't want other people to hear, they should have the conversation when they're alone." Time to change the subject. She was probably partly right, but sometimes other peoples' conversations were interesting, as was people-watching, although I felt odd staring at strangers unless there was a camera between us. "That was James before. We can visit them at home, but I'll have to text first, in case mum and baby are sleeping."

"They still haven't named her?" asked Liv.

Beren shook his head. "I called James this morning, and no. How long can babies go without having a name?"

I shrugged. "I have absolutely no idea."

My scalp prickled, and not with magic.

Uneasiness cascaded over me. Someone was watching. I was sure of it. I turned this way and that. Nope, no one inside Costa was so much as glancing my way. My forehead tightened. I looked at each of the windows to the footpath and road beyond. When I reached the last window, the sensation dissipated.

Liv stared at me. "Are you okay? You look a bit pale."

I created a bubble of silence. "Something was weird. It was like someone was watching me. When I looked out the front window, the feeling disappeared."

"You sure you weren't imagining it?" Liv asked.

"Well, there's always the chance I could've been. It was just a feeling. I didn't actually see anything out of the ordinary. But I'm pretty sure someone was watching me." Was I being paranoid?

"It's a possibility, Lily, but I don't sense any immediate danger. Are you okay to stay, or do you want to go home?" Beren asked.

Since the feeling had disappeared, it should be fine, and I wasn't going to let some creepy snake person ruin my double-chocolate muffin and coffee. "Nah, let's stay and finish. I'm sure it's nothing." I smiled for emphasis.

As we chatted, the people from the table behind me got up to leave. The woman pushed her chair back into mine. A sorry came from behind me. I turned. "Not a problem." I smiled and hid my surprise. It was the woman who'd kicked us out of the plastic surgery thing yesterday. She was with a grey-haired, slim man I recognised as the cosmetic surgeon from the internet article.

She said nothing about recognising me, turned, and left with her dad. I turned back to Liv and Beren. "Did you see that? She pretended she didn't know us."

Liv's forehead wrinkled. "Isn't that the woman from yesterday at the hall?"

"It sure is. Why doesn't she like us? We didn't do anything to her. Seriously? First she kicks us out; then she pretends not to know us."

Beren swallowed the last of his cheese-and-ham croissant. "Maybe she's just not a people person. Or maybe she does recognise us and doesn't want to have to apologise again for kicking us out?"

Hmph. I hated being ignored, but Beren made some good points. "Maybe she wouldn't let us in yesterday because she wants him to slow down. You heard what she said."

Liv looked at me. "Well, can you blame her? He's getting on. And maybe she's sick of working for him? She might just want to see him enjoy life. I know my parents are always their happiest when they've just returned from holidays. Dad used to take hardly any holidays, but the last few years, Mum's made him take six weeks off. They go somewhere different every time. What's the point of working till you die?"

"Looked to me like he loves it. I guess sometimes it's hard to let go." Case in point, disappointment flooded me as I finished the last of my muffin. If only I could eat another without putting on four pounds. Beren and Liv had both finished their brunch. "You guys ready to meet the baby?"

Liv's smile was wide. "You bet! I've been looking forward to this since she was born. Let's go!" She quickly stood.

As we walked home, under a cold, blue sky, we chatted about the baby, all thoughts of being watched forgotten.

CHAPTER 11

Monday, bored because everyone was at work and I was confined to the house, I practiced a few spells from my grimoire. Admittedly, one was totally useless, but now there was one very confused squirrel who'd briefly worn a tutu. I only made it wear it long enough to get a photo. Hopefully the squirrel would think it had all just been a bad dream. If not, I was probably going to hell. I magicked some nuts for it to the bottom of the tree. After gathering some of the offerings, it flicked its bushy tail at me, which I was taking as thanks rather than sod off.

When I'd run out of energy to perform magic, I sat with my iPad and read. As much as I was tired, I couldn't help listening out for Will at the reception-room door. It was close to 5:00 p.m., and I was eager to hear how the interviews had gone. Each small noise had me sitting up straight in the armchair, looking over the back of it towards the door like a meercat on high alert for birds of prey.

Each day we didn't figure out what was going on was another day someone might die. Why was practically every investigation against the body-count clock?

The fire crackled and popped, and I jumped… again. Bloody hell. When did reading get so stressful? When the person is waiting on news, that's when. At least I knew Millicent and the baby, as yet unnamed, were okay. If James didn't get his act together soon, I was going to give the baby a name, and there'd be nothing he could do about it.

I sat up straight, ears pricked. That was definitely the reception-room door. I jumped up and hurried to the hallway. Will met me there and swept me into his arms for a long-awaited hug and kiss, and by kiss, I didn't mean a peck on the cheek. When we came up for a breath, I asked, "How did it go?"

He rubbed a thumb gently across my bottom lip. "Do we have to talk about this now? I'd rather prefer to keep doing what we're doing." His dimples made a swoon-inducing appearance as he gave me his gorgeous boyish grin.

"Well… as much as I'd prefer not to, I've been waiting all day to hear what happened."

He sighed. "All right. Come on." He took my hand and led me into the living room, where we sat in front of the fire. "Would you like a coffee?"

"I won't say no." I grinned.

"Yeah, I didn't think you would." He magicked us each

a cappuccino, then created a bubble of silence. "We still have their parents, some other family members, and friends to interview, but we managed to speak to quite a few people today, including their boss and two of their best friends. They both worked at the local vet and were studying veterinary science."

I sank back into my armchair, sad. "That's even worse. They were animal lovers who wanted to do good in the world."

He nodded. The sorrowful look in his eyes matched how I felt. "Yep. Anyway, we have a few avenues of further enquiry at this stage. We've yet to interview one of the other vet nurses at their work. Apparently the three of them didn't get along. There was one witch working there—a vet—and he mentioned that the other staff member was a witch too. The boss and other staff have alibis. The only one unaccounted for is that witch, Julianne. Next, we spoke to Ellie Fisher's twin brother. He's obviously not a witch, and he said the girls did everything together. The only out-of-the-ordinary thing they'd done lately was go skiing in Switzerland for a week with friends. We spoke to Ingrid Braun's aunt, and she had nothing much to add. Everyone we've spoken to so far says the girls were happy and doing well. Neither has trauma in their past, their parents are all still together, and there aren't any drug or alcohol addictions. So far, no dark secrets. We'll just have to keep digging."

I couldn't believe I was about to suggest this, but as painful as it was to use my talent, the family and friends of these young women were going through so much worse. If I wanted to be a decent human, I'd do what I could. "I know there was no need for me to take photos after Ingrid died because Agent Johanssen had seen everything, but maybe I should. Just in case he missed anything."

Will's brows drew together as he looked at me. Then he peered out the window. "It's cold and dark, and you might see something else that shakes you up. Do you really want to do it?"

"I don't have a choice. I need to do what's right, Will." The nightmares would disappear eventually, and maybe they'd get worse if I didn't figure this out.

Will pulled out his phone and looked at something. When he was done, he met my enquiring gaze. "Weather app. There's a storm coming down in Dover. Dress warm and take an umbrella. Maybe wear your wellies."

"Consider it done." I clicked my fingers for fun, and there I was in a red ski jacket and black wellies, a large, black umbrella leaning against my chair. I smiled.

Will nodded and returned my smile. "Nice work." He made no gestures, but his lips moved silently before his thick coat and umbrella appeared. His feet were also covered in black wellington boots. He created a doorway and gestured for me to go first. Through I went, to the disgusting public toilet by the roadside. As gross as it was, I stood just inside the doorway as rain pounded deafeningly on the roof. Outside, reflecting illumination from the streetlight, the raindrops were tiny white lasers shooting to the ground in a shower of icy sparks.

So uninviting.

Will had to raise his voice to be heard over the cacophony. "Uber'll be here in five."

I found myself practically shouting. "Are they going to think we're weird? I mean, who the hell goes to the cliffs in this weather in the dark when you can't see the view?"

"Does it matter what they think?"

"I don't know. Maybe." I wanted to come up with a good reason we'd be going now, of all times. And there it was. I smiled. "Floral tin in the kitchen, please come to my hand; this I do command." I nodded. Not bad rhyming. Not perfect, but maybe I was getting there. Even better, the colourful, small, empty tin appeared in my hand.

"What the hell's that for?"

"It's the empty tin from specialty tea I bought Liv. The container's so pretty, she decided to keep it."

"Yes, but why do you have it now?"

Headlights flooded the road, and tyres crunched on gravel as our Uber pulled up in front of the toilets. "Just look sad." I schooled my features. He shook his head and rolled his eyes but did as asked.

We jumped into the car, and the Uber guy asked, "Where are you headed?"

Will answered, "White Cliffs, thanks."

The guy twisted around to stare at us with incredulity. "Are you mad?"

My closed lips trembled, and I blinked as if about to cry. "We have to scatter my uncle Michael's ashes. He stipulated this date and place, and we couldn't get here earlier." I held up the tin and sniffed.

His eyes widened momentarily, and he shook his head. "Okay, then." He turned back around, put his blinker on, and pulled out onto the road. Will looked at me, one brow raised. I shrugged. What did he expect on such short notice? I thought it was super clever of me. You just couldn't please some people. I hugged the tin to my chest and did my best to look glum about poor Uncle Michael.

It didn't take long for the Uber to reach our destination. We got out and opened our umbrellas. Even with the downpour, I could taste the salty air. We each cast protection-from-rain spells, and I magicked the tin back home. "Goodbye, Uncle Michael. We'll miss you."

Will gave me a "you've got to be kidding" look. "Come on, you nutter, let's get going."

I lit the way with my phone. It was slow going, as we couldn't jog for fear of twisting an ankle in the limited light. Thank goodness my past-seeing magic didn't work that way. The latest jump had happened during the day, so I'd see it all. Hmm, come to think of it, that wasn't good. I sighed. Watching people's last moments was torturous, especially because there was nothing I could do to change it. I supposed I had to focus on the future, the one where we quickly caught the perpetrator.

We reached the spot of doom. I stopped. Dangling around my neck was my trusty Nikon. I raised it. My stomach tensed as I drew on my power. "Show me the last person who jumped off the cliff."

Brightness. Blue sky with high, white puffs of cloud. It wasn't video. Thank God.

We were standing well away from the cliff edge, so the whole scene was captured in my lens. Agent Johanssen stood a little bit back and to the left of a small group of people, one of which was a slim, young woman. Her dark, straight hair cascaded down her back from under a blue beanie. While those standing near her were laughing and taking selfies, she stood ramrod straight, staring out to the English Channel. Whether she was actually seeing or looking blankly, I would never know.

"Show me two seconds from this photo." I closed my eyes and opened them again. The scene was the same. Either my request hadn't worked—maybe my magic couldn't be that specific—or she'd waited longer to leap. "Show me five seconds from this photo." Shut eyes. Open eyes.

My pulse pounded in my throat, and I couldn't help the anguished "No!" that blurted out. I snapped a shot, then stepped closer—not too close, mind you. I hadn't forgotten about that fatal drop. I zoomed and took a shot of Agent Johanssen, his face contorted, mouth open wide, as he likely screamed at her to stop. His arms were bent, preparing to sprint.

But it was too late.

The smiles on the bystanders' faces had twisted into shock and horror. I knew how they felt.

Ingrid had stepped off and was falling. Already, her legs were cut from view, her arms above her head, her beautiful hair blown upwards as she dropped. I clicked and clicked.

"Hey! Hey!" Will shouted.

I started and lowered my camera, then frantically looked around. "What. What is it?"

But he wasn't there to answer. Someone was walking from the path towards the cliff edge. They had peeled off about twenty feet from us. Will had dropped his umbrella and was sprinting towards them. I'd say it was a pretty safe bet that they were here to jump. This was crazy. It was as if someone had trained their own human-lemming hybrid army. Why would someone do this?

What if Will needed help? I magicked my camera back home and threw light on the situation with an illumination spell. I didn't want Will going over the edge in the dark. And whoever this person was, Will or Ma'am could wipe their memories later. As unethical as it was, sometimes it was unavoidable.

The dark shape was a man, almost as tall as Will. His steps were hurried, determined.

Knowing there might be some spell bounceback, Will didn't use magic—he'd even dropped his protection-from-rain spell, probably so he didn't look weird with the rain bouncing off an invisible shield. Will stopped in front of the man, squinting against the downpour and blocking his path to the cliff. But the stranger tried to walk around him. Will stepped to the side, blocking him again.

I edged closer, just in case.

The man stepped to the other side; so did Will. "Hey, buddy. Stop. Talk to me. What's your name?" No answer. Then, out of nowhere, the man faked to the right, then dodged left and ran. Will turned and leapt after him.

Adrenaline shot through my system, and my heart raced. "Careful, Will!" I shouted, ready to cast some kind of spell to save him if things went terribly wrong. Problem was, everything was happening quickly, and it was something I couldn't plan for. What if I cast the wrong spell?

The man darted towards the edge, Will on his heels. I stood still, tensed, ready for… I didn't know. Icy air scraped down my throat with each nervous, shallow breath, then plumed in my witch light on the way out. Silence had possessed the clifftop, except for the thudding of rain slamming into the ground and the rasp as my breath sawed in and out.

The stranger was only eight feet from the edge. Will dove towards him.

"Will!"

He took out the man's legs, and they both fell forward, towards the cliff. I wanted to shut my eyes, but that wouldn't change anything. If he went over, I'd never forgive myself. I edged forward, pushing through my fear, which was like a dam of thick molasses between me and the cliff.

They rolled around on the ground, the stranger throwing random punches, which Will expertly, or maybe luckily, avoided. Will was on top of the man now, astride his stomach. And all this time, the stranger said not a word, but he grunted as he writhed and bucked, trying to dislodge the man I loved.

Will leant forward, arms crossed forearm over forearm, and grabbed both sides of the man's coat collar, then pulled his hands together. Oh, wow, he was choking him. We weren't meant to kill him. What was the point of that rather than just letting him jump? What was he doing?

After a few seconds, the man stopped flailing. His arms dropped to the ground. Will, panting to catch his breath, jumped off him and grabbed his ankles. He quickly pulled him towards me, away from the edge.

Thank God Will's okay. I honestly didn't know what I would do if I lost him. Okay, so if he chose to leave, I'd figure out how to deal because I wasn't some psycho stalker, but if he died, I'd be inconsolable.

By the time Will reached me, the man was coming to. What if he took off again? Will was tired. Yes, he was trained for this kind of thing, but what if he wasn't as successful next time—it was obvious the man would just keep trying till he was airborne. Plus, I could see how valuable it would be to actually have someone to question, maybe even magically poke about in their mind to see what was going on. Not to mention saving a life.

Will quickly looked at me. "Lily, follow me to the PIB." His magic tingled my scalp as he built a doorway around the rousing man. Then they disappeared.

I extinguished my magic light and followed.

CHAPTER 12

As soon as we landed in the reception room, our charge was back to full force. He wrestled Will. I managed to dodge the warring men and reach the intercom. I pushed the buzzer multiple times, like pedestrians at traffic lights who think pressing the button more than once is going to make things happen faster. FYI: it doesn't.

Both of the chairs crashed against the wall as they barrelled through them. If we weren't so worried about spells bouncing back, we could have had this handled straight away. Will seemed to be getting the upper hand, and so he should, being a trained professional, but the guy had terror on his side. I was sure he was freaking out about the miraculous change in venue.

Finally the door opened. Boy, was I happy to see backup. "Gus, you're back! Can you help?"

"Yes, Miss Lily." It seemed as if Gus's self-imposed work ban was over. As much as I hated his questionable conversation topics, I'd missed him. He stepped in and pulled something from his belt. "Give me his back and hold him, please, Agent Blakesley." Will struggled with the red-headed man. There was no way this guy was turning around. Just because we couldn't put a spell on him didn't mean I couldn't help Will. I drew on my magic. "Give Will the physical strength to do what Gus has asked. Make Will strong enough so we can see the guy's arse." Oh dear. The things I'll say to make a rhyme.

The man fought harder, but it wasn't working. Will grabbed the man's right wrist with his right hand. Pulling the man's arm straight, Will then stepped to the guy's right side, turning to face me at the same time. He hooked his left arm over the captive's right, just above the elbow, and levered his arm until the man screamed. Getting compliance, Will turned them both around to face the wall. He dropped the man's arm and tried to force him flat to the wall, but he resisted and got Will in a headlock. Will lashed out, grabbed the man's trousers, and pulled, hard. A monumental ripping sound echoed off the walls as Gus fired the gun-looking thing he'd pulled out earlier.

Gus tasered him, hitting him square in his snow-white bum cheek. The guy stiffened and fell to the floor, Will now free. Once the redhead was on the floor, face first, Gus pressed the taser to his calf. I slammed my hand over my mouth as the poor man screamed and screamed. This predicament wasn't even his fault, although, being tasered was way better than dying at the foot of a cliff.

Gus turned it off, removed it, and pushed Will out of the room before joining us in the hallway and locking the door. The man lay face down on the floor, groaning, his bottom still exposed. Oops.

Will looked at me. "What the hell just happened? I felt your magic, and then I was stronger."

"I spelled you so you could get the upper hand." I didn't mention asking to see the man's bottom, because that's not exactly what I'd meant to happen. I wasn't a pervert… honest. I was just really bad at rhyming, especially under pressure, and they needed him to turn around. I'd have to be more careful next time—magic took everything literally. "So now what?"

Footsteps clacked down the hallway. I turned. Angelica strode towards us. "What's going on?" Of course Gus would've sent her some signal to come fix things. He was a smart man.

Will explained our predicament. She looked through the glass into the room. "Why's his derriere exposed?"

Will's answer held a note of accusation. "Lily's overexuberant spell."

"But I helped you. Why does it sound like you don't approve?"

"I appreciate your help, and I'll admit that it was the difference between getting him to turn around so Gus could use the taser, but you should've warned me, Lily. It's dangerous to cast a spell on someone and not expect retaliation. What if I'd had my return to sender up?"

Oh. I'd forgotten to check. That fact was obviously written all over my traitorous face. Angelica folded her arms. "You need to be more careful, Lily. How many times have I had to say that?"

"Well, normally I would've checked. I mean, what's the worst thing that could've happened? I would've been stronger. That's all."

Will gave me a stern glare. "Or you might have found yourself in there, trying to get the man turned around. What did you say to create the spell, exactly?"

I shrugged, then mumbled, "Give Will the physical strength to do what Gus has asked. Make Will strong enough so we can see the guy's arse."

"Lily Katerina Bianchi!" Angelica's mouth was forming the "o" in poker face. "You really need to be more careful."

Will's serious face was ruined by one corner of his lips, which tried to break rank and smile. He held his hand out, and a pair of jeans appeared in them. "We'll have to get him to put these on."

"But how are you going to get them in there. What if he attacks you again?" I nudged next to Angelica and looked through the window. The man was standing, his back against the wall. At least fabric covered his crotch. Thank goodness for small mercies. His expression was dazed with a side of crazy eyes. He was likely questioning his sanity right now too. It was probably scary to be locked in a strange room when you last remembered being on a clifftop in a storm. Okay, *probably* was a silly word to use. Who wouldn't lose the plot if something like that happened to them?

Ma'am grabbed the pants from Will. "We can only try and explain what's happening. We'll mindwipe later, but for now, we need to delve into his brain, see what spell has been used. To do that, we'll have to earn his trust. I'm going to construct an invisible shield around myself. It takes a lot of energy, so I'd prefer this didn't take too long. I'll come out for a break if I need to—just be ready. I'll lock the intercom-communication button down so you can hear what's being said."

The energy of her magic electrified my scalp, then subsided. She opened the door and entered. Hopefully the guy wouldn't be aggressive with a woman. I could understand feeling threatened by Will's imposing form, but even though Ma'am was likely even more dangerous, she only looked like a fit but normal middle-aged woman.

It would be awful if they had to taser him again.

Her voice was gentle yet firm with cheery undertones. "Good evening. I'm Angelica DuPree, the head of operations here. I'd like to apologise about the tasering. We didn't want our staff harmed. I understand that you find yourself in quite confusing and distressing circumstances. Would you like to put on new jeans?" She held them up, and he eyed them warily, his gaze darting from them to her face and back again. "We're not going to hurt you in any way. I promise. My agents found you at Dover. You were going to jump off the cliff. Is that right?"

He hugged himself and stared at the pants. Ma'am

moved ever so slowly to hold the jeans out in front. When he didn't flinch or become aggressive, she took a small step forward. Her magic caressed my scalp, and I checked out her aura. She'd dropped the protection spell. "Please take these. Your other ones are ripped." I held my breath, waiting. If he attacked now, she'd be in trouble. And what was wrong with his chin? Had it been broken in the scuffle with Will? The man had a very rigid, square jaw, but where it came to a point at his chin, it was more like the harsh angles of an irregular parallelogram. The right side of his jaw stuck out further than his left; the line forming his chin and joining both halves of his jaw were angled rather than straight or rounded.

The man looked into her eyes and warily took a step forward, holding his hand out. Ma'am had to take one more step towards him, and then the jeans were in his hand. He scurried backwards, placing his back against the wall once again. Instead of putting the jeans on, he held them low in front of himself. "Are you an alien?" His Scottish brogue was rather attractive. I was such a sucker for an accent. But even with his gorgeous accent, I slammed my hand over my mouth to stop the laugh that wanted to escape. Oh dear. The poor guy. He thought he'd been beamed up into a spaceship. Who could blame him, though? One minute he's running across a field in Dover, the next he's in a sparsely furnished white room.

Ma'am shook her head. "No. You're at a government facility on Earth, still in the UK, in fact. My accent should give that away. Can you tell me your name?" He shook his head. "Can you tell me why you want to kill yourself, then?" I sighed. This was beyond frustrating. Life sure was hard when you couldn't use magic. I had a new appreciation for what normal police went through.

He seemed to consider her question, then shrugged. "Ah dinnae ken." Huh? What the hell did that mean?

"You don't know?" Ma'am's voice was ripe with disbelief. "Surely there's a reason. No one does it for no reason. Have you been depressed?"

"Och, no that ah can remember." His forehead furrowed, and he scratched his head. "Ah just wanted to, aye."

"So, would you say that you're happy we stopped you jumping off the cliff?"

He shrugged and blinked. He was at least partly confused. We were likely getting closer to obtaining hard evidence that these people had been compelled to kill themselves.

"Can you tell me when this urge started?"

He gripped the thick red hair on the crown of his head with one hand and pulled his head down till his chin rested on his chest. He dropped his hand and looked up at Ma'am. "Maybe a week ago?"

"Just out of nowhere?" He nodded. "Right. Do you understand that I want to help you?" He shrugged. "Do you want me to leave you in here by yourself for a minute so you can get changed?"

"Um, och, aye. That would be good. Thank you."

"When you're done, just press that button there."

Ma'am half turned and pointed at the intercom button. She was wise not to put her back completely towards him. He might get the urge to hurt her and escape. Ma'am opened the door slowly and stepped out, gently closing it, probably so as not to startle the man. We all moved away from the window to give him some privacy. The door was locked, so there wasn't anything he could do.

Will folded his arms and looked at Ma'am. "What do you think?"

"We need to get him to open up to us. If he doesn't comply, we'll have to use an old-fashioned method to knock him out and carefully prod inside his brain. Not knowing the spell that's been used is tricky. His aura tells me there is some kind of spell, but it's embedded deep, and the symbol is hidden."

"Excuse me, Ma'am."

"Yes, Lily?"

"He didn't look like he was in pain, but did you notice his weird chin. It didn't get broken in the kerfuffle with Will, did it?" Maybe whatever spell he was under meant he didn't feel pain or fear?

She pursed her lips, thinking. "I don't think it's broken, but I did notice it. Interesting...."

The intercom buzzed, and the Scot glanced out the window. Ma'am went to the intercom and spoke to him. "I'd like to keep talking to you, but I'd prefer to do it somewhere more comfortable, like my office. If we go there, do you promise to come quietly? We just want to get to the bottom of what's going on. We think you may have been hypnotised. Once we've asked you some questions, we'd be happy to take you home. We can even order you some food if you're hungry." Hmm, that wasn't a bad idea: framing it in concepts he could understand.

My stomach heard the word food and gurgled. Will smirked. I patted my offending body part. "Can we just order some food anyway? I'm starving."

Ma'am turned and glared at me. Oops. "Lily, I have delicate work to do. I think it's best if you go home. Will and I can take it from here."

My cheeks burned. When would I learn to keep quiet? I'd complain about my treatment, but I was the one who didn't want to be an agent. Why didn't I think of going home in the first place? Sure, I'd helped Will get the guy here, but other than that, I was done. "Um, yeah, I'll just head home. I'll send those photos to your phone, Will."

"Thanks." He gave me a wink when Ma'am had turned back to the window. At least he still loved me.

I turned to Gus. "Great to have you back. We missed you."

His expression was sombre. "Thank you, Miss Lily. It's good to be back."

"I'll see you all later." I moved down the hall enough that the Scot couldn't see me before I made my doorway and went home—he'd had enough drama for one night. I tried not to get excited, but maybe we were close to finding an answer.

CHAPTER 13

During the night, I was vaguely aware of Will slipping into bed but quickly fell back into a deep slumber. When I awoke the next morning, he'd already left. Something must be going on. That man might still be at PIB headquarters, and Will had to hurry back. Whatever was keeping him away, I crossed my fingers that we were about to discover what all these people had in common.

Needing something to do while I had my morning cappuccino, I checked my emails. Ooh, two photographic job enquiries. One was a wedding happening in June, the other a woman who showed cats and wanted professional shots of her animals. I grinned. What would she do with those photos? Did they swap business cards with the other cats at shows? I could just picture it. A large ginger cat saunters up to a sleek Siamese and puts a business card on the table in front of her. "You have the most gorgeous blue eyes. Call me, floofy baby," he says, "and we'll catch up for a bowl of milk." As soon as he walks away, she briefly looks at the card before swiping it off the table. I giggled. Despite people thinking I was strange, being able to amuse myself meant I was rarely bored.

The woman getting married had sent her phone number. As it was after nine, I thought I'd call rather than email. She sounded nice enough on the phone, and we agreed to meet in a week so we could go over what she was after. She'd already seen my portfolio online and loved it, so while she admitted she was also talking to one other photographer, she really wanted to meet with me before she decided who to go with.

The other email didn't include a phone number, so I emailed, asking for more details. When I was done, I checked Facebook and Instagram to see what my Sydney friends had been up to. There my besties were, at the beach on a hot summer day. And another selfie of them with some cute guy at a bar. A sharp pang of homesickness reverberated through me. I wouldn't leave here—almost everyone I loved was here—but I did miss my old, carefree lifestyle. Going where I wanted when I wanted. And I definitely missed the warmer weather and my swims in the surf. Maybe when we finally shut down the snake group, I could take Will, Beren, Liv, and Imani to Sydney and show them my gorgeous hometown.

Ooh, there was a new message in my inbox. I clicked on it. It was from the cat lady. Okay, she had a name: Fern

Davis. Fern sent me her address and was wondering if I could come today or tomorrow. She'd also seen my photos on my website and claimed she had to have me take the pictures. There was some TV work coming up, and she needed to have the photos for her cat's agent so she could send them onto the casting director. I smiled. So, it wasn't too far off what I thought. She was even willing to pay me cash at the door before I started. Talk about an urgent job.

Before I could make an appointment, I had to check whether Imani was free. She and Will were so busy at the moment, I doubted she'd be able to make it, but I might as well check. I texted her, knowing she could possibly be in an interview, although she probably had her phone on silent anyway. Still, I liked to be considerate, just in case.

I've been asked to do an urgent photography job. It will take one to two hours from start to finish. Do you have time today or tomorrow? If not, that's okay. Just thought I'd check. Lily xx.

I shut my laptop, took my phone into the living room, and looked out the window at the grey sky and cavorting squirrels. I didn't mind cold weather, but now the snow had melted, and after seeing those photos of my friends, I was over it. Bring on spring! Maybe I could check out some of the beaches in France or Italy when the weather warmed up? Hmm, that was a cheery thought.

My phone dinged with a message.

I can spare an hour today, at twelve, and maybe an hour and a half tomorrow between ten thirty and twelve. Can you do the shoot in two lots?

Not sure. I'll check. Thank you so much! I'll let you know ASAP.

I got straight into my email and gave those times to the woman. I just said that I was super busy and that's when I could squeeze her in. I also asked her to confirm the package she was after—I had five to choose from on my site. She emailed back within five minutes, confirming what she wanted and asking if I could please come today. I confirmed the appointment and price, and that was that. The universe was obviously feeling generous today. I'd take it. It wasn't often getting a job was that easy. I texted Imani back and confirmed with her.

Right. I needed to make sure I had everything for the shoot. I raced upstairs and picked out what I'd need—camera, extra flash, photography umbrella, roll-down background, three different lenses, tripod, reflector, and a stick with feathers attached to grab the cat's attention. The racing wasn't necessary; it was just that I was excited to be doing something. Sitting around the house lounging wasn't my thing, at least not all day. I loved tiring myself out with stuff and then enjoying the relaxing afterwards. It felt kind of dishonest to relax when I hadn't done anything.

Once I'd magicked everything into Angelica's car, I read until Imani arrived. When she knocked on the reception-room door, I jumped up. You knew you were a bit pathetic when going to work was the most electrifying thing to happen in ages. But to be fair, freelance jobs weren't easy to come by, and I was slowly racking them up.

I opened the door and gave her a quick hug. "Hello! Thanks so much for doing this."

She smiled. "I had some time between interviews, and hey, look how happy it's made you."

I locked the reception-room door and headed to the front door. "Let's not waste any time. The house is ten minutes from here. I think you can just pop away from my car as we leave. That will save you some time."

"Sounds good."

I slid into the driver's seat and shut the door. My hackles rose, and I stiffened. It was the same feeling of being watched as in the café. As soon as Imani got in the car, I locked the doors.

"What are you doing?"

Glancing out each window in turn, I said, "Just being careful. I had a weird feeling." It had gone, but my mouth was dry. Was it paranoia, or was there something to it? With everything that had been going on, it could be either. I took a deep breath and released it slowly. "It's probably nothing. It's gone now."

Focussing on the job ahead and shutting out the what ifs, I appreciated the dry roads as we made our way to Tandridge Lane. I made a bubble of silence. "How are the interviews going? Did Will say anything about last night?"

"Last night went well. Ma'am found out that Ryan, our captive Scot, had surgery about six months ago to make his chin more masculine. Will and I led with that question today when talking to the family of the girls who worked at the vet. Interestingly, both of the young women had surgery as well. One had her boobs done, the other one had liposuction and what they call a body lift or something. They all had it at the same place."

I sucked in a breath. "Does that mean we're almost there?"

"Maybe. We still have to look into the surgery. We have no idea why this is happening. Without a motive, it's difficult to be sure about anything."

"But what about the signature on the spell? Surely that will help pinpoint what's going on."

"We had to be very careful. He gave permission for our 'doctor' to touch him. When he probed in his brain for the spell, it unravelled and dissipated before he could get a read on it. The damn thing was buried deep. I have no idea how the witch managed it. You'd need someone to stay still for a fair amount of time to get it done."

I sighed. How would they ever prove who did this? "Does that mean Ryan won't try to kill himself again?"

"It looks that way. Will said Ryan confirmed the urge had disappeared. We have an agent covering him, just in case, but Ma'am and Will dropped him off at home, Ma'am wiping his memories of that night just before he got out of the car. They told him they'd found him wandering near a pub, and he told them where he lived. He bought it, apparently."

I put my indicator on and turned left. "So now what?"

"We're interviewing the other victims' families, just to confirm whether they'd had plastic surgery and where. Once we do that, we'll have to get a warrant and obtain their patient records, then put this thing together, provided it's the same plastic surgeon. The first three victims had all been to the same one."

"Interesting. But why would they kill their patients? Wouldn't you think they'd want them to live and come back again for something else?"

She shrugged. "I don't know. I really don't. The alternative is that someone hates the surgeon and is killing his patients out of spite, or maybe someone has some weird hatred towards plastic surgery in general. Hmm, it could even be a competing surgeon. Too many options."

"Nothing would surprise me, unfortunately. But that doesn't help the people who are dying." We drove in silence for the last few minutes of the trip. "Ooh, here it is. Bardwell House. It looks like a normal house to me. Do a lot of people name their houses here?"

"You could say that. Or, rather, they're already named. The original owners, one, two, or three hundred years ago would have named their houses, and I guess people with more modern houses like the idea of it."

"Fair enough." There was nowhere to park on the street, so I pulled into the driveway and drove up to the garage door of the single-storey bungalow.

"I didn't think to ask, but do you want me to be your assistant, rather than cast a no-notice spell on the contents of your car? Is the client a witch?"

"Ah, good question. I have no idea if she's a witch or not. You may as well come in. I could always do with an extra pair of hands." I smiled.

Imani helped me get everything out and carry it to the

front door. Before I could knock, a woman with short, curly grey hair opened the door. She was about my height and wore a short-sleeved shirt, long tartan skirt, long socks pulled up, and lace-up black flats, which kind of looked like school shoes. "You must be Lily. I'm Fern. Please come in." I utilised my other sight, just to check her status. Non-witch. Fine.

"Lovely to meet you, Fern, and thanks. This is my assistant, Imani."

Imani gave her a nod and smile, and Fern stood back to let us through. She wrinkled her brow. "I didn't realise you were bringing someone, but that's fine. You can take your things into the next room, through that door." She followed us to a sparsely furnished living room. An armchair with footstool, small TV, side table, and plush-style pink cat house huddled on one side. The other side was bare, except for a couple of country scenes on the wall. "You can set up just there, sweetie."

"Okay. That would be perfect. I have a backdrop I can use." I got to work setting things up and directed Imani as she helped. When we were done, Fern called in the star.

She momentarily left the room. Her voice filtered in, coming closer. "Miss Periwinkle, darling. Come on, precious." She made kissy noises, then appeared, a Siamese cat following, and I swear, she had a supermodel strut.

"What a gorgeous cat." I crouched and made kissy noises of my own. "Hello, pretty girl. You have the most amazing blue eyes."

Fern beamed. "She's been best in show the last five

we've entered. At the last national cat show, a talent scout was there, and that's why we need the photos now. She might be in a very big movie soon."

"How wonderful," I said. Imani stood to the side, a small smile playing on her face. She wasn't much of an animal person, not that she disliked animals, but she likely thought this scenario quite amusing. I slowly stood, so as not to startle Miss Periwinkle. "Let's get started."

Miss Periwinkle was an obedient cat, which made my job so much easier. We were done within forty-five minutes. I showed Fern some of the photos and explained how I would retouch them.

"Do you think you could have them ready tomorrow?"

I knew they were urgent but talk about pressure. I supposed I had time this afternoon to edit them. "Yes, sure."

She beamed. "Thank you so much, Lily! Oh, and here's your money." She handed me an envelope, which brought back memories of the night before my birthday, when the father of the bride gave me a tip for a job well done. He'd been the first casualty I'd seen through my lens when he'd appeared see-through, only to die the next day. That had been the last time I'd been happily ignorant of witches. Not that I wasn't happy now, but there was something to be said for a simpler life.

Despite the awkwardness, I counted the money. I hated this part of it. At least with direct debits, I didn't have to call the client's honesty into question by counting things out. "Thank you, Fern. It's all there. I'll make sure you get those photos later tonight."

"You're a doll. Thank you."

Imani and I packed up and left. Yay for an easy day. By the time we returned home, I'd forgotten all about the weird being-watched creepiness, and I edited the photos and sent them to Fern by dinner time.

My instincts were rarely wrong. One day I'd get it right. One day.

CHAPTER 14

The next day at twelve, we were called to a meeting with Ma'am at the PIB. This must have been the slot Imani had thought she was free. Luckily we did the photography job yesterday.

As per normal, Ma'am sat at the head of the table. Her grey bun was tight, clothes so neat, you'd think she'd just bought them. I looked down at my own black jeans and red jumper, then blew some hair that was tickling my nose away from my face. I was so not agent material. Oh, crap, was that a spot of coffee on my jumper? Yes. Yes it was. Why was I even surprised? Okay, to be honest, I wasn't.

I sat between Liv and Will. Beren and Imani sat opposite. James still wasn't back at work, and I knew Mill was grateful he was there to help with things. He was doing all the housework and getting up to bottle feed once a night. My brother was awesome.

Ma'am cleared her throat to get our attention. "Good morning, team. As you know, Agents Jawara and Blakesley completed many interviews yesterday and this morning. We now have a clear lead: Dr Joe Ezekal. Every suicide we're investigating had some kind of surgery or cosmetic enhancement at his practice. Most had it in his London surgery before he moved here."

I sat up straight. "Oh my God. He's the guy that had the open day." I turned to Liv. "Remember on Saturday, and they wouldn't let us in?"

"Oh, yeah. That's right."

Ma'am eyed me. "Next time, Lily, please put up your hand if you want to interrupt." I clenched my teeth as I tried to resist an eye-roll. Oops, failed. Ma'am raised a brow and increased the disapproval in her stare. I put up my hand. "Yes, Lily?"

"They had an open day on Saturday at Westerham Hall. We went past to check it out, and they wouldn't let us in."

"Did they say why?"

"It was only one woman, really, but she said they only worked with people who really needed it, and none of us needed it. I'd usually say awesome ethics, but I don't believe that for a minute. It's rare that any business would knock back money."

"Well, dear, I do agree with this woman that none of you are in need of it, but I also agree with your latter assumption. So there must be another reason, the clue to which lies in our victims." Huh? I didn't get where she was going, which probably wasn't unusual. I was the amateur after all. I imagined she got paid the big bucks for untangling these messes before others.

Will leaned forward. "I agree." He turned to me. "And before you get upset that you're out of the loop, I'll fill you in." Alas, poor Will, he knew me well. "All our victims are non-witches."

"Do you think they're only killing their non-witch victims because they don't like them? Kind of like, take their money, then eliminate them?" That didn't sound right, but the snake group was all about hurting non-witches. "Are they linked to RP?"

Will shook his head. "I don't think so, and I don't think they hate non-witches, but we don't know the doctor. We'll need to investigate further. It could also be someone else, someone who's trying to ruin the doctor's practice, and maybe that person hates non-witches. Still, there is that matter of them not wanting to deal with us. We have to assume it's because we're witches, which discounts the theory that someone outside of the doctor's sphere is hurting these people."

A piece of paper appeared in Ma'am's hand. "Here's the warrant to search the doctor's premises. I also want you to take him in for questioning, please, Agent Blakesley. Take Agent DuPree with you."

Will and Beren stood, and Will said, "We'll get right on that, Ma'am." He took the piece of paper from her and looked at it, then showed it to Beren. "Coordinates are on there."

"Thanks." Beren handed the paper back to Will.

"Handy. The surgery is two minutes' walk from our landing spot. See you there." They both made their doorways and left.

Ma'am rested her forearms on the table and looked at Imani. "I have another case that we're close to an arrest on, but my team could do with the assistance. I want you to relieve Agent Parker for the rest of your shift. Here are the coordinates." Nothing happened, except a tingle of her magic, so she must've transmitted them via mind picture.

Imani stood. "Will do, Ma'am." She nodded at us. "See you later, ladies." Then she was gone.

Ma'am turned to us. "Liv, how are you going with those research items I gave you on the Morrison case?"

"I'll need another three hours or so. There are a couple of things I'm waiting for from our contacts at the police."

"Okay, good. If you can have them to me tomorrow, I'd appreciate it. If there are any delays, let me know."

Liv smiled. "Yes, Ma'am."

Ma'am asked her about a few more things, so I zoned out and stared at the shiny tabletop. It was so clean. Did it have a spell on it so it would never get dirty? Hmm, maybe I should invent that kind of spell, although, if it existed, then maybe the spell wouldn't let anything sit on the table, and that would be silly.

Ma'am's phone rang, and I started. Maybe I needed to concentrate on an anti-jumpy spell. I certainly needed one.

Ma'am answered it and frowned. "Why are you calling me so soon?" She listened. "You're sure?" She heavy sighed.

"Right, well, come back. I'll have to think about this." She hung up.

I risked getting in trouble, but I asked anyway. "Was that Will?"

"Yes."

"What happened?" I tensed, waiting for the rebuke to mind my own business.

"There's been an unfortunate turn of events. The good doctor and his employees are all non-witches."

Liv's eyes widened. "What? But how could that be?"

Ma'am looked at her hands for a moment, then back at Liv, but didn't answer. I put up my hand. "Yes, Lily? And by the way, if I'm not already talking, you don't need to do that."

Oh, for goodness' sake, I couldn't win. As far as I was concerned, better to be safe than sorry, so she was getting the raised hand from now on. "But what if they hired a witch to do their dirty work? Can't you at least question them?"

"It's too risky, dear. Maybe they're the target of someone else. We can't investigate because they're non-witches. It's not in our jurisdiction. And at this stage, we have nothing tying the magic to them, or even a particular witch."

"But the victims are tied to them. And we know there's been some magic use."

Ma'am shook her head. "Yes, but we haven't linked magic use to every victim. I'm going to have to hand this over to the regular police, although, I'm going to give us twenty-four hours to find the link before I do."

"So now what?" Liv asked.

Ma'am fixed her predatory gaze on me. "We need to deploy our secret weapon."

And I bet I could guess what… or *who* that was.

Me.

CHAPTER 15

Just before 5:00 p.m., Will and I snuck into the London Orthodontic Clinic. It was a four-storey building within a row of terraces. How could this be a medical practice? It looked more like a home. London couldn't help but be stylish. In Sydney, the building would have been a modern glass and steel structure—cold, new, sterile. Although, I supposed you wanted sterile when you were having surgery, but the old buildings spoke of knowledge, wisdom, and skill.

We hid in the toilets, cloaked by no-notice spells, waiting for the place to be locked up. This was the building Dr Ezekal's practice had been in before he'd moved to Westerham. Now it housed, as the name suggested, an orthodontic clinic. The tongue-tingling scent of fluoride saturated the air. I shuddered. I'd had two fillings in my life, and whilst not the worst experience ever, the remembered drill vibrations and horrible tastes made me cringe.

I looked at my phone: 5:15 p.m. I glanced at Will with a "Do you want to check out there now?" look. He shrugged, motioned for me to stay, then crept to the bathroom door before disappearing into the hallway. I slipped my phone back in my pocket and waited, straining my ears for any sounds of confrontation.

After what seemed like forever, he returned, speaking quietly. "I've swept the whole building. Everyone's left for the day, and I've magically disabled the surveillance system. We're good to go."

I whispered, "So why do we have to speak quietly?"

"Habit. It's best to uphold these precautions, just in case. It would be bad to accidentally break it at the wrong time." He made a good point. Once an agent, always an agent.

He led me into the hallway and around the ground floor. "There are storage and consultation rooms. We don't have to worry about the storage areas, of course. We'll start with the consultation rooms before going upstairs where there was a surgery and some recovery rooms. The recovery rooms have been converted to dentists' rooms now. Don't let that throw you off."

"Don't worry. Not much throws my magic off. I just ask it for favours, and it does the rest." The process was so easy, too easy, in fact, and gave no hint of the consequences I often experienced after seeing things I didn't really want to see.

We entered the first consultation room, a carpeted

space with a large, shiny mahogany desk, and black leather chair. In front of the desk were three white-fabric chairs with yellow daisy motifs. When I lifted my camera to my face and asked to see Emily Armond, the scene changed. A smaller desk had replaced the current one, and the chair became white rather than black. Only two chairs sat in front of the table, and they were green. Sitting in one of the green chairs, her back to me, was Emily Armond, the French woman who was our first known victim. Sitting behind the desk, a kindly smile on his face, was Dr Ezekal.

I wandered around the desk, taking shots from different angles. The hope on Emily's face at whatever the doctor was saying flooded me with sadness. If not for this, she'd probably still be alive. Why had all these people ended up dead?

I lowered my camera, then brought it back to my face. "Show me what kind of plastic surgery Emily got." The scene changed. It was the same day—they both wore the same things—and the doctor was showing her boob implants. He held one in each hand, maybe showing her different size options? I took a couple of photos and lowered my camera. I lifted it again. "Show me Alice Baker and why she was here."

This time the doctor was sitting on the edge of his desk, leaning towards Alice, who had on another outfit that was a riot of colour. Toucans happily fluttered across her short-sleeved, loose-fitting dress. She'd paired it with bright-yellow sandals. Her head was angled up, and Dr Ezekal held her chin in place whilst drawing on her Roman nose with a purple marker. I hoped he had something to get that off with because it didn't look like he was about to operate.

I walked around and photographed Alice from the other side. Her nose was normal size, and certainly nothing you'd worry enough about to cut into. Letting my camera hang from the neck strap, I turned to Will. "Alice Baker, the woman with the colourful clothing—she had a super small, overly pointy nose, didn't she?" I was pretty sure I remembered it correctly, but I wanted Will's confirmation.

"She did. Why?" I brought up the photos and handed him the camera. His brows drew down. "This looks like he was only supposed to fix the bump. Why did he make the tip ridiculously small?"

"I don't know. I'm wondering if we should check to see if she ever complained. Should I look for files?"

He handed the Nikon back. "Yes, but I'll call Olivia too. See if she can unearth any complaints to the medical board. If there are none, we may have to assume she was happy with the job."

I found that very hard to believe—that she'd be happy. Her nose when she died looked like you could stab people with it, and how did she breathe out of such tiny nostrils? I pushed those thoughts out of my mind and lifted the camera. *Show me evidence of Alice Baker's complaint over her nose.*

Nothing changed. Damn. Time to move onto our next potential victim.

Our first male victim, Andrew Porter, was next on my list. I asked my magic to show me why he'd been here. This time, Andrew stood next to the doctor as he pointed to a drawing he'd pinned up on the screen behind and just to the left of his desk. The drawing of a torso had areas circled: pecs, biceps, six-pack area. My mouth dropped open. He wanted implants there? I shuddered as I clicked off some shots, the icky sensation of having foreign bodies under my skin creeping me out. The lengths people would go to, to change their appearance. I shook my head and handed Will the camera. He looked at the images, shook his head, and handed the camera back to me.

Despite knowing the reasons people had visited him, it didn't give us a motivation for the suicides or murder. Hmm. There was something I was missing. Going with the nose thing, I decided to ask for an after shot. "Show me the finished product of Andrew Porter's plastic surgery."

Shirtless, Andrew sat on the bed that was against one wall, a grin lighting up his face. Dr Ezekal examined his handiwork. Oh. My. God. What the hell? I moved closer and took a few shots. One pec implant was at least half an inch lower than the other, and his six-pack implant looked like a fake superhero costume. And what could I say about his balloonish, bulging biceps that were way out of proportion to the rest of his skinny arms?

I was on a roll with the information so didn't stop to show Will. "Show me why Ellie Fisher was here." She stood in front of Dr Ezekal in her underwear, her arms held out to the sides, parallel with the ground. Her slim body was weighed down by inches of excess skin. Skin fell in a large fold from her stomach to touch the tops of her thighs, and loose skin drooped from her upper arms. She must have lost a lot of weight, and good for her, but solving one problem had left her with another. I couldn't imagine how self-conscious she must have been.

I flicked the camera off and on again. "Show me the results of Ellie Fisher's surgery." My old friend nausea was back, sloshing around my stomach, splashing up towards my throat. A woman dressed in black pants and blue shirt stood next to him, her face bland, as if she didn't want to give any reaction. I sucked in a breath. That was his daughter! The same woman who'd told us to leave, the same one who'd had the argument with him in Costa. Maybe she did hate her job? She certainly didn't look overjoyed to be there.

The doctor, though, wore a much different expression to his daughter. How could he be smiling, pride shining from his eyes at the *good* job he'd done?

A massive, thick scar ran like a crazed smile from hip to hip. The jagged purple track pulled the skin together unevenly, so it was noticeably looser and wrinklier on her left side than her right, and one arm still had a dangle of flabby skin. Her stomach was also weirdly lumpy, like badly made custard. Maybe he'd done some liposuction and had missed sections?

Her smile told me she was happy with the job. The only logical answer was that she was excited to be rid of most of the excess skin, even if the job wasn't nearly as good as it could've been. How much had she paid? I shut my eyes. "Show me the receipt from Ellie's payment to the doctor." I opened my eyes and pointed the camera at the desk, assuming a piece of paper or laptop would appear. It was paper, in her hand.

Twelve thousand pounds. That wasn't cheap, especially for a student and vet nurse. You'd expect a bang-on job for that. This was more "bang," as in a messy explosion. Ire sizzled in my veins, and I clenched my teeth. I was sensing a theme here. But why was everyone happy with the substandard results? The answer to that was probably where we would begin to find our answer.

I showed Will the pictures. His nostrils flared. Anger flickered in his eyes. "Talk about a botched job. How is this guy not in jail or at least struck off the medical register? Actually, has anyone even checked that yet?"

I shrugged. "Don't ask me. It's the PIB's investigation."

He grabbed his phone and dialled. "Olivia, yes, hi. Can you do me a favour? I need the medical registration for Dr Ezekal, and can you look into whether he's ever had any complaints against him? …okay, thanks." He turned to me. "Take the photos for Ingrid and our Scottish friend; then we'll go to headquarters and send Ma'am the pictures."

"How are we going to explain these photos?" If agents who didn't know my special talent looked in the file for this case, they'd surely wonder how we'd gotten them.

"Don't worry. No one else will see them."

I took the rest of the photos, and then we were done. I should've been happy—we didn't get caught trespassing—but as I stepped through my doorway to the PIB, I was anything but.

CHAPTER 16

The next morning, I slid out of bed, bleary-eyed and with a combination of an emotional and magic hangover. I'd been using my magic consistently lately, and with all the sadness and confusion of the current PIB case, I wasn't feeling the best. I would've been looking forward to an easy day, but we all had our brains working overtime trying to find the missing link in the case. Ma'am said she wouldn't need my magic today, so at least I'd be able to rest.

I dressed, magicked a coffee, and sat in front of the fire. Outside, raindrops blurred the windows. Another cold, rainy winter's day. I snuggled my back against the chair and cradled my coffee to my chest.

Finally fully awake after finishing my coffee, I magicked my laptop from my room to myself. My physical laziness knew no bounds today. At this rate, I wouldn't recover my overall energy in a hurry. I needed to curtail the magic use.

Argh, emails. A few junk ones. Delete, delete, delete. Oh, Fern had emailed. Please don't be a complaint.

Hi Lily, I wanted to thank you again for the wonderful job. Also, you may be missing a lens. I've found one that I'm sure is yours. It has Nikon 24-120 mm in gold writing on the side. I hope you don't mind picking it up today as I'm going away. We have a show in Germany tomorrow. We fly out this afternoon. I'll be home until 2:00 p.m. If you can't make it, let me know so I'm not worrying.

Fern.

How had I managed that? But, really, was I surprised? I'd had a lot on my mind, and when dealing with animals, you had to be super focussed, plus I'd been on a strict time schedule. Whatever. I needed that lens, just in case, meaning I was missing it now I knew it was gone. My camera equipment were my babies, and the various pieces were expensive. It had been stupid of me to forget it. But stupid *was* my middle name.

I texted Imani to see if she could come with me.

I've got twenty-five minutes I can spare. Will that do? That was cutting it fine, as without traffic it would take almost fifteen minutes each way, and it was raining, which slowed things down, but I'd just be running in and out, and surely I'd be safe driving the last five minutes home by myself if I had to.

Yep, that's fine. When can I expect you?

Instead of a message on the screen, there was a knock on the reception-room door. I smiled. She didn't muck around. Because I was on a tight time frame, we jumped straight in the car and went.

Halfway there, Imani made a bubble of silence and said, "When we get back, Ma'am wants you to join us. I think she's decided where to go next in relation to the *botched* case."

Of all the insensitive names she could've picked. "Are you kidding?"

"Why would I kid about that? She wants you there."

I rolled my eyes. "No, I mean calling it botched. Those people deserved way better than what they got. Since we can't confirm that they were all spelled, do you think that's why some of them killed themselves? I mean, wouldn't you at least complain or try to sue if someone did something like that to you?"

"I would think so, but not everyone has the finances or confidence to take it to court."

"If it's not that, then what?"

Imani didn't answer. We were both lost in thought for the rest of the trip—she gazed out the window, whilst I strained my eyes on the road, which was fuzzy through the speeding windscreen wipers that struggled to keep up with the downpour.

I pulled into Fern's driveway, parked, and looked through the maelstrom towards her front door. "Yuck." I'd forgotten a raincoat, but, hey, I was a witch. I smiled and magicked my raincoat on. I put my hand on the door handle and turned to Imani, saying in my best spy-movie voice, "I'm going in." She laughed as I flung the door open and leapt out.

As soon as I reached the front door, Fern opened it. "Oh dear, look at you! Come inside." She stood back as I entered.

"I'm so sorry I forgot my lens. As my dad used to say, I'd forget my head if it wasn't screwed on."

She laughed. "It's not a bother. Come on through, and I'll grab it for you." She led me to the living area we'd taken the photos in the other day. She grabbed it off the small table and handed it to me. "Here you are."

"Thank you." I smiled, but then my hackles rose. I spun around as that shuddersome feeling I'd been having on and off engulfed me. A hulking man in a black T-shirt and black leather jacket stood there. I reached for my magic and other sight at the same time. He was a witch all right, and his return to sender was up.

Fern screamed, and the man flicked his hand. Abrupt silence. *Thud*.

Grinning, the man grabbed my wrist. Pain lanced deep into my bones. I tried to pull away, but he was too strong. My wrist stung, the skin heating until it burned. I screamed at the pain. What was wrong with me? I needed to get away. The oily stench of burning flesh and wool coated the back of my throat. I was wearing my hiking boots, so I drew my foot back and slammed it into his shin. *Get away*.

His grip tightened, his grin twisting to a sneer.

As much as I tried to show nothing, I winced as my arm

burned and my breath came in short pants. Heart racing, I drew on my power and created my own return to sender.

The searing agony stopped.

I kicked him again, satisfied when anger flared from his eyes. I drew my foot back to go again, but he released me and stepped back a pace. He looked at my wrist, then back at my face, made a doorway, and disappeared.

I turned. Fern lay on the ground, unmoving. Damn it. Not again. An innocent person dying. Or was she innocent? Had I left my lens here, or had she surreptitiously kept it so I had to come back? I knelt and felt for a pulse. Nothing.

When the man appeared, she'd shown no surprise, and she must've seen him. I hadn't seen a no-notice spell in his aura. But why? And if he wanted to hurt me, why leave when things had just gotten started?

Imani's magic tingled across my scalp. The front door slammed open, and she flew through the door, murder in her eyes. She stopped when she saw me; then her gaze fell on Fern. She stared at me. I put my hands up in surrender. "It wasn't me. Some guy appeared, burned my wrist, then left. He killed her, although I'm not sure how." I stood.

Imani cocked her head to the side, likely considering what I'd said. Indignation stormed through me. Did she think I was lying? Why would I lie about that? She slapped her hands on her hips. "Don't give me that look, love. Of course I believe you. I'm just trying to figure out what the hell's going on. I felt the magic, and the car doors locked. I couldn't get out. As soon as I could, I rushed in. Her gaze moved to my hip, and her forehead wrinkled. "Are you hurt?"

"I was, but I'm okay now." I lifted my right hand. "He grabbed it, and it felt and smelled like it was burning, but it doesn't hurt now." I looked at it. My eyes widened.

What the hell?

I swallowed rising nausea, and tears swarmed my eyes. I had no words. I locked eyes with Imani. Horror had slapped her poker face to the kerb, jumped on it, and was dancing a jig of triumph. "Are you going to say anything?" Her silence made everything worse.

She shook her head. "Geez, love, I'm sorry. I just… I'd never lie to you, and, well…."

Yep, so this was bad. I licked two fingers and tried to rub the black markings off. Nothing budged or smeared. I scratched it, dug my nails in till it hurt. The lines and curves were as dark as before. Unless Ma'am could remove it with magic, it was permanent. I swallowed and blinked back tears. I wasn't a tattoo person, yet the worst one of all circled my wrist.

A snake.

Despite my fiercest intent, the tears fell. What did this mean? Could they spy on me, control me, stop my magic? Was it going to slowly kill me as a type of torture?

Imani slid her arms around me and tried to soothe me with comforting words. But there was nothing she could do to make it better, short of chopping that part of my body off.

My life would never be the same again. I just knew it.

CHAPTER 17

I sat on a bed in the PIB sickbay, surrounded by Ma'am, Will, Imani, and James. Doctor Finnegan held my wrist as he pulsed power through the tattoo and whispered different spells. Beren held my other hand, his eyes closed. A faint trickle of his power leaked into me as he observed how my magic and the tattoo reacted. I yawned. Three hours had passed since Imani and I had returned to the PIB, and Ma'am had ordered me in here. And all because of a bloody camera lens. How had I been so stupid?

Doctor Finnegan swayed and stumbled backwards. I sucked in a breath. Luckily, he stayed on his feet. Ma'am looked at him. "I think that's enough for now. It's imperative that this analysis is finished ASAP. Can we resume in an hour?"

The slim doctor, who was about Ma'am's height but

about ten years younger, took a deep breath. "Yes, Ma'am. Of course. I'll just have something to eat. I should be as good as new in an hour." We all knew that was a lie, but he was putting on a brave front. Magic really drained a person, especially at the level he was using it. "It will take another thirty minutes or so; then I'll be able to give you accurate results."

"Righto. I think we could all do with something to eat and a break." She looked at me. "I'll have something brought up for you, Lily. I want you to stay here, and remember…" She pinched her forefinger and thumb together and ran them across closed lips, indicating I shouldn't talk about anything we didn't want RP to hear. Until we sorted this tattoo thing out, I was damaged goods, a potential source of information leakage, even surrounded by bubble-of-silence spells. It really sucked to be me right now. I nodded. "Good. I'll see you all back here in an hour." Ma'am turned and left.

Beren sat in a chair next to Imani. James and Will were sitting at the foot of the hospital-style bed. Everyone stared at me. No one was smiling. Great. I leaned back into the pillow and closed my eyes. My stomach grumbled, reminding me I'd had nothing to eat since this morning. A chair scraped against the hard floor, and Will said, "What do you want, Lily? I'll grab you something from the café."

I opened my eyes. "Um…." I was hungry but I wasn't. "Surprise me."

His brows drew down. "You hate surprises."

"I'm too tired to think, and even though my stomach is screaming for food, my brain is saying it doesn't care."

Imani put her hand on my forehead as if taking my temperature. "Are you coming down with something, love?"

"Yeah. I have a bad case of snake tattoo." I sighed and scowled at the ugliness on my wrist. The snake itself wasn't ugly, as far as snakes went, but it reminded me of RP, and everything that went with it. Had they tattooed my parents like this? Or had they just killed them without bothering?

James shook his head. "I'm sorry, Lily."

"Why? This isn't your fault." A scythe of guilt cut through my heart. James should be at home, spending precious time with his wife and baby, not here blaming himself for my mess.

"I should've protected you."

"You can't be everywhere saving me from everything, especially not my own stupidity. I should've put my return to sender up earlier. We'll figure it out, and it will all be fine." I put on the fakest of fake smiles. James answered with one of his own.

"Why don't we go get some food and bring it back?" Will said to James. "Come on." He walked to the chair at the end of my bed and patted my brother on the back.

James stood and looked at me before turning his gaze on Beren. "What do you want?"

Beren leaned back in his chair, exhaustion darkening the skin beneath his eyes, and his blond hair mussed up from running a hand through it. "Burger, chips, and a chocolate milkshake, thanks."

Will turned to Imani. "And you?"

"Caesar salad thanks, love, and a black tea, one sugar."

The guys left. I shut my eyes in the silence that expanded until everything unsaid was a crushing weight on my chest. What would happen? Would my friends cast me out, exclude me from everything because I was a spy risk? I couldn't blame them, and really, it shouldn't be their burden to choose. I didn't want them to feel guilty. Maybe I'd have to make the decision. Would going back to Australia be an option? Even if I managed to sneak away, would this tattoo make me easily trackable?

Feeling sorry for myself was pathetic, but I was doing it. A tear wriggled free and slid down my cheek. I bit my tongue to stop the rest. Crying was not going to fix anything.

"Lily?" Had Imani been watching me?

I took a deep breath before opening my eyes. "Yes?"

"You're not in this alone. Do you remember what I said to you at the funeral that day?"

I did. Well, not word for word because my memory was unhelpful at the best of times, but she'd said I was special, that I was important in what was to come. Back then, it made no sense, but now we knew about Regula Pythonissam, I could see what we'd need help fighting. But what if I was now their weapon to use? "Yes, I do. But things have changed."

She shook her head, and a gentle smile softened her face. "You're going to be the difference in whatever's coming. This"—she pointed at my wrist—"changes nothing.

And, even if it did, I wouldn't abandon you. I'm in this with you all the way. Not just because you're special, but because you're my friend, and I care about you. No matter what comes, I'll be by your side." She grabbed my hand in both of hers and squeezed.

Beren, on the other side of the bed, touched my shoulder. "Ditto." I smiled at him being such a guy. As few words as possible, but the sentiment was there.

"Thank you. I love you guys, but I don't want to drag you into the abyss with me. Maybe I should disappear for a while."

"You can't!" Imani's stern face was back, her brown eyes brooking no argument. "If you try, I'll hunt you down and stick to you like an oyster to a rock. There is no escape." She waggled her eyebrows and smiled.

As down as I was, the corner of my lips twitched. It was nice to be loved. But, unfortunately, it didn't change the fact that I was even more of a liability now than I was. At least before, I was only a danger to myself, but now I was risking the security of everyone I came into contact with. I swallowed, and dizziness gripped me. "What if they can control me? What if they can make me hurt you?" The flicker of worry in Imani's eyes was there and gone so quickly that I could've, maybe, convinced myself I was imagining things, but I wasn't into fooling myself.

"Look at me, Lily." Beren touched my arm. I turned and met his gaze. "The tests aren't finished yet, but from what I've seen, this tattoo is likely just that. There is a small amount of magic in it, but it's possible they just want you to have a constant reminder they're there and waiting for you. I can't guarantee that, of course, but we'll know more when Dr Finnegan completes his assessment. Try not to worry until we know what exactly we're dealing with. Okay?"

I supposed it was only an hour or so I had to promise to not worry for. Not that I wouldn't be stressing, but I'd just be able to keep quiet about it and put on a brave front. Sixty minutes, that was it. Totally doable. "Okay."

Will and James returned, which was great as it would stop further conversation. Hopefully they were in the mood to eat and not talk. My surprise lunch consisted of lasagne and salad. It smelled delicious, and it was, but I could only stomach half of it. I'd eaten enough to stop the grumbles from my midsection without having to slog through eating everything when I didn't feel like it. Everyone was still eating when I finished, so, yet again, I shut my eyes and relaxed back into my pillow.

I must've fallen asleep because someone was holding my shoulder and gently shaking me. "Huh?" I opened my eyes to James and his crooked smile.

"Hey there, sleepyhead. Sorry to wake you, but Dr Finnegan is ready."

"Oh, of course. Sorry." I wiped dribble from the corner of my mouth, and James laughed.

"Some things never change." He winked and returned to his spot at the foot of my bed. Beren took my hand, and Dr Finnegan wrapped his hand around my wrist. Here we went again. I was grateful, though. Both the doctor and Beren were exhausted, as was I, but they weren't giving up until they found an answer. The least I could do was be a patient patient.

For the next thirty minutes, I alternated between staring at the ceiling, occasionally meeting the worried gazes of Will, Ma'am, James, or Imani, and closing my eyes. The warm hum of magic from Dr Finnegan didn't hurt, but it was a little uncomfortable, the vibration an unsettling sensation that hummed up and down my arm and occasionally to my stomach where my portal to the river of magic resided.

I tried not to think about what they would or wouldn't find and instead considered our latest case. Why had no one complained about the botched surgeries? And why would they all jump off the cliffs at Dover? It wasn't a coincidence. The magic we'd noted had to have come from somewhere, but where? And we hadn't been able to confirm magic for all the victims. What were we missing?

The magic stopped flowing, and both the doctor and Beren released their grips on me. I paused before opening my eyes. The verdict would show on their faces. Even though they were agents, I assumed the doctor wasn't as good at poker faces as Ma'am, and Beren tended to show more emotion than the average agent, at least where his friends and family were concerned.

My heart galloped as I opened my eyes. This was it.

Ma'am had joined us while I'd had my eyes closed. She stood with her arms folded. "So, Doctor, what's the verdict?" Her even tone belied the fact she was asking a question that could determine my fate. I clenched my fists to stop them from covering my ears. If I lost self-control, I was likely to start saying la la la la la la la la la to block it all out.

Dr Finnegan shared a *look* with Beren, but I couldn't read either of their faces. I turned my gaze to Will for support, and he gave a small nod, as if to say it was all going to be okay.

But was it?

I imagined a fluffy squirrel giving me a drumroll on a tiny drum hanging from his neck, his little arms frantically striking the drumskin with the sticks. But it wasn't enough to make me smile. When squirrels didn't do it for me, I knew things were bad.

Dr Finnegan focussed on Ma'am. "It's not as bad as we thought, but it's not great either." My stomach dropped, and the food I'd just eaten wanted to make a break for it. "To start with, the tattoo has been embedded with magic, so there is no way to remove it, except working out a counter spell. Whoever created this has woven an extremely strong confusion spell with it. It's impossible for me to follow the spell pattern without being redirected or disoriented. I imagine that whoever did this almost killed themselves in the process. A lot of time and power went into it." So Beren's initial assessment was wrong, unless he'd just been trying to make me feel better.

Ma'am didn't sigh, but her nostrils twitched. "Okay. What else?"

"There's a tracker in there, which also has a confusion spell, but it isn't as strong as the one protecting the tattoo. Also, we know most of the tracking spells, if not all, so it might just be a matter of going through the process of using an undo spell for each one until we find the exact spell. They may have tweaked one slightly, which could make our job all that much harder. In any case, I would say Lily is going to have to live with that spell for a few days to weeks." The doctor swallowed and stuck his finger in the collar of his shirt, pulling it away from his neck. Oh, great, here it came. The worst news of the lot. "The third spell… it's… challenging."

Ma'am's forehead wrinkled. "In what way?"

The doctor winced, as if he was about to get in trouble. "I've never seen it before. Maybe Agent DuPree could give you more of an idea." Ma'am's raised eyebrow indicated she was less than impressed.

Beren hurried into the awkward silence. "It's not something I've ever seen before, but I have a couple of theories. I recognise elements of things in there, but nothing clear, and as with the other spells, this one has confusion over it. I can tell you what it's not. It's not a listening spell or something to spy visually. It can't read Lily's mind or stop her magic. But there are threads of a connection spell and something that's waiting… if that's even the right word. Some of this spell is hiding because it's yet to be activated. It may need another spell to make it work as intended. It's like it's the first part of a spell. I also see traces of a binding spell."

None of this sounded good. I had to ask. "Can we chop my arm off from just before the tattoo?"

Imani sucked in a loud breath, and James and Will's mouths dropped open in horror. I didn't bother to look at

Beren. He likely had the same reaction. Only Ma'am seemed relatively unscathed by my suggestion. "No, dear, we won't chop off your arm, or even part of it. At least not yet. Maybe as a last resort, but I'd like to avoid that if we can."

Right, so it was a possibility. I suppressed a whimper. All those days I'd thought were the worst ever, and I'd been wrong, wrong, wrong. This was clearly the worst day of my life, only to be superseded by the day they actually chopped my arm off. How was I going to deal with it? Would I have phantom pain forever and end up addicted to painkillers? Plus, it was my right hand. I'd have to learn to write and take photos with my left hand. Would Will still want to date me if I was sans one hand? Thank goodness I had magic to help with putting my hair in a ponytail and tying my shoelaces. Oh my God, how was I going to take the lid off a takeaway cup and lick off the chocolate while holding the cup at the same time? It wasn't like I could use my magic in public. There were so many things my right hand did to help my left.

"Lily? Sweetheart, hello." Will had changed places with Beren and was waving his hand in front of my face.

"Oh, hello. Sorry. I spaced out."

He smiled. "I could see that little brain of yours racing to places you shouldn't be going. We have the best witch minds here, Lily, and we'll get to the bottom of this. Also, just in case you were wondering, I'd be fine with you having one hand." How did he know what was going on in my brain? I checked. Yep, my mind shield was up. "I know you." He waggled his eyebrows and grinned, his sexy dimples appearing. I sighed. He was so cute.

Someone cleared their throat. I looked up, into James's disgruntled face. "Lily, how many times have I told you that I don't want to know what goes on in your personal life. I don't even want a glimpse."

"How old are you, James? You're a father now. You're going to have to get used to this stuff. When baby Bianchi grows up, there'll be no ignoring things." I smirked. "When is she getting a name, by the way?"

Ma'am sighed the sigh of a long-suffering teacher. "Enough! I have some thinking to do. William, take Lily home. Beren and Imani, get back to work. James, we have some things to figure out. Can Millicent do without you for a couple of hours?" Gee, she must be rattled if she'd reverted to first names.

"Yes, she can. This is important. If she needs help, her mum is around, but the baby's been good, to be honest."

"Right, you come with me; the rest of you, do as you're told." She turned and gave the doctor a firm nod. "Thanks. If I have any other questions, I'll let you know. Make sure you're on call for the next couple of days."

"Yes, of course, Ma'am." He gave her a half bow.

I put up my hand. Ma'am stared at me, her gaze hard. "What now?"

"Um, so is it definite that they can't hear what we say because of the tattoo?"

She stared at the doctor. He grabbed either side of the stethoscope hanging around his neck and pondered, although why he had one of those instruments when he was a witch, I had no idea. Maybe it was all part of the doctor look. "Pretty positive. There was nothing that looked like any traditional eavesdropping spell, even in the bits we could decipher. But I can't guarantee it. Who knows? They may have come up with radically different spell constructions we're ignorant of. We'll have to do more testing. Beren's got the spells in his memory now, at least the parts that weren't hazy, and we'll recreate them tomorrow and start working through solutions. But, as I said before, it's going to take some time. We'll probably need another session with Lily. Sometimes the confusion spells aren't consistent, and we may be able to see different parts of the spell we couldn't see today."

"There's your answer, dear. Don't talk about anything regarding any cases or other matters you wouldn't feel comfortable discussing in front of our enemies. Now, if that's all, James and I have work to do."

James gave me a hug, and they left. Will took my hand. "Are you ready to go home?"

I shrugged. "I suppose so. But what's happening with the case we were working on?" I could generalise if I had to. Just because I was having a disaster didn't mean everything else stopped. We needed to figure out why Dr Ezekal's patients had become lemmings.

"That can wait half a day. I'm pretty sure Ma'am's time frame for handing it over has changed. This… *situation* needs priority, at least until we form a plan. Don't worry, Lily. We'll get everything sorted."

The back of my throat and nose tingled with impending tears. "But more people are going to die. Has someone else jumped off today? And if they haven't, I bet they will. We need to get records of all his patients. Can we protect them somehow, like what happened with Ryan?" As far as I knew, his urge to jump had dissipated after our interference.

Liv, who'd been busy and as a non-witch not privy to what was going on in here, ran through the doorway. "Lily!" She rushed to the bed, practically shoved Will out of the way, and threw her arms around me. "James just told me what's been going on. Are you okay?" She leant back to look at me.

"Ah, kind of. We're just not sure what this stupid thing does." I held up my arm so she could see my wrist.

Her eyes widened. "Oh." Yeah, *oh*. Her reaction, whilst not unexpected, caused my heart to sink further. At this stage, I was mired in hopelessness. Would this tattoo eventually kill me? Would it make me do something I didn't want to do? I just wanted it off, gone. A flame of anger heated the quagmire of despair in my chest, and bubbles of resentment rose to the surface. Whatever this tattoo did, RP was going to pay for putting it there. Every last one of them. As soon as I knew what had happened to my parents, that was it; I was going to go feral squirrel on them—yes, squirrels were small, but I reckoned they were fierce when they got mad, just like me.

I wasn't a giver upper. I was going to fight this. Okay, so I still had to find where they were and plan how to go about their destruction, but if I was desperate to destroy them because of what they'd done to my parents, now I was doubly committed. No one forced me to live my life in fear, and how dare they try.

"Lily? Are you okay? You look really angry." Liv's gaze was on my face rather than my wrist.

"Oh, yeah, I'm fine, and yes, I'm really angry. No one does this and gets away with it." I held my wrist up again and spoke loudly to it. "Hear that, snake people? You don't scare me. I'll be coming for you one day soon, and you're going to regret ever messing with me and my family." Everyone stared at me open-mouthed. "What? Am I supposed to let them intimidate me?"

"Ah, love, they probably can't hear you." Imani's mouth quirked up on one corner. "But I love your spirit."

I looked at Beren. "But it's a possibility, right?"

"Unfortunately, yes. If they can hear, I'd love to see the looks on their faces. Imani's right—just keep being you."

"Thanks."

Liv sucked in a breath. "Oh, there was a reason I came up here. I was asking about you because I'd tried to text and couldn't get you or Will. James told me where you were and what happened. Anyway, there's something I have to tell you urgently."

"What? And don't give too much detail, just in case they're listening," said Will.

She looked momentarily confused but then opened her mouth as she pulled an "ah, I get it now" face. "Ryan, the Scottish man from the other night. He's just been arrested at Doctor

E's office in Westerham for aggressive and disorderly conduct. He was there yelling and threatening staff. They called the police, and one of my contacts in there passed it on, as I'd asked him to keep an eye out for anything in relation to the doctor."

I swung my legs over the edge of the bed, ready to leave. "Did they say why he was angry?"

"He said they messed up his jaw, and he wants them to pay to have another doctor fix it."

Will and I looked at each other as realisation dawned. "So that's what the spell does," I said.

"Exactly!" said Will.

Imani looked at me. "Oh, my lord, yes. Now it makes sense."

"What are you all talking about?" Liv's brows drew together.

I answered, "No one's been complaining about the doctor's dodgy operations because they didn't notice. Someone spelled them so they would think they looked okay. That must be it. But who?" I looked at Will. "You said none of them are witches."

He pressed his lips together. "They're not. And we need to confirm this with living patients. I think we have to start there. I'm going to talk to Ma'am. Have someone police the clifftop and physically apprehend anyone who's going to jump. If we use no-notice spells, we could walk next to people without them being on guard. We'll throw them through the doorway, like we did last time."

Imani folded her arms. "Good idea. So we have motive

but not opportunity. Could they have hired someone to do it?"

Liv wrinkled her forehead. "But non-witches aren't supposed to know about you. When I researched the doctor and his employees, there were no ties to witches in any of their family or close relationships. Going through phone records and things is going to be a nightmare since they run a busy surgery. It could take weeks to weed everyone out."

I sighed. "Now what?"

"I think we start with what I suggested. We need to confirm our hypothesis first."

In all the drama, I'd forgotten about Fern. "What happened with Fern? Are you going to investigate her death?"

"Her murder, you mean." Imani gave me a "you should know better" look.

"Yes, that."

She nodded. "Agents arrived just after we left. It's a PIB matter now."

"Okay." Had she been in on it, or had she been mind controlled by RP? I had no idea if they could even find out. "What's going to happen to her cat?" That poor Siamese cat would miss her mother.

Imani answered, "Her niece is taking her."

"That's good." Sadness, so much sadness. Why couldn't things just be nice for a change?

Will stood. "Come on, gorgeous. It's time to go home and rest. I'll take you; then I'll come back here and have a chat with Ma'am. How are you feeling?"

"Tired, unhappy, but I'll live… at least for now, unless the tattoo has other plans for me." I narrowed my eyes at the small snake entwined around my wrist, daring it to strike me down. Nothing happened. Hopefully, it would stay that way.

"It's been a long day, and I'm almost done, Lily. You'll only be by yourself for an hour or so; then I'll be home." Liv smiled.

I swallowed as a thought struck me. "What if the tattoo can make me hurt other people? Liv, you won't have any way to defend yourself."

Beren stood, frowning. "We didn't see anything like that in the spells, but you're right. We don't actually know. Liv, I don't think you should be alone with Lily until we confirm it." And just when I thought my day couldn't get worse….

Her face fell. She hugged me again. "I'm so sorry. I'd ignore that advice, but if something happens, I know you'll never forgive yourself."

"You're right. I wouldn't. Don't worry; I'll see you tonight when Ma'am gets home at seven… if she's even home then. Maybe you should go stay with your parents or Beren?"

Beren and Liv looked at each other, Liv shy and blushing. "I couldn't impose on B. That's okay. My parents will be happy to have me."

"Why not? Just for a few days. It'll be fun." Beren waggled his eyebrows and grinned.

I smiled, in spite of the reason this was happening. "I think you should. Look at it as a holiday. I'd feel better if I knew you were safe, and if Beren can't keep you safe, no one can. Don't feel bad. Okay?"

"I can't promise that. Can you come see me for lunch here tomorrow?"

"Yes, I totally can, and I don't mind the cafeteria food. Twelve?"

She nodded. "Sounds good. I'll come round with B tonight to get my stuff too, so I'll see you then."

"Okay. In the meantime, I'm expecting Will can chat to Ma'am and update me later as to what's happening."

He rubbed my back. "Definitely. I'll try and get home early today, maybe bring some paperwork so you don't have to be by yourself."

"Thanks, but you don't have to. I'll be fine." Ah, the lies we spouted.

His smile was gentle. "I know you, my little Aussie witch, and you'll be the last one to say you need something. I want to be there, even if it only makes the smallest difference. I love you." He kissed my forehead, and I sank against his chest. God, I loved this man. How did I get so lucky?

My voice was quiet. "Thank you."

"Okay, loves, I have to get going. I'll join you at that meeting, Will. I'll speak to Ma'am, see if she can meet with us in fifteen minutes in her office. I'll text you if that changes."

"Sounds good. Thanks." Will looked at me. "Let's go."

Imani gave me a hug, and Beren waved a sad floppy hand. I shrugged and gave him a "what can you do?" face. "See you later, guys."

Will took me home, made sure I was settled, then left. I sighed. Damn snake group. Even though they'd been spying on me before, it creeped me out that they knew where I was for sure. Goosebumps rippled along my arm. Stupid tattoo. Being alone with the snake ink and my thoughts was not going to be fun.

As usual, I was right.

CHAPTER 18

By 9:30 p.m., no one had come home. Exhausted, I went to bed. Sleep was a great way to escape my thoughts. I woke at eight to find a gorgeous man slumbering next to me, his arm slung over my waist. It was hard not to sigh. He tended to keep himself clean-shaven for work, but stubble darkened his face. So sexy. I smiled. It wasn't possible to ever get sick of waking up next to Will, and I hoped I'd never have to experience being without him again.

"Hey, creepy lady. Stop staring at me." He opened one eye, then the other, and smirked.

Damn. Busted. "How did you know?"

"I'm very attuned to things around me. That's why I'm an awesome agent."

"That's what you think. Awesome is a matter of opinion." Before he could counter and I lost my nerve, I asked,

"What's on the agenda for today?" Firstly, I wasn't sure I really wanted to know, and secondly, would he refuse to answer on account that I was now to be left out of the loop? Bloody tattoo.

"A few things. I'll let Ma'am explain. She's going to have breakfast with us this morning. In fact, it's probably time to get up." He yawned, then pulled me closer to him. "Although I don't much feel like getting out of bed just yet."

I snuggled into his chest. "Neither do I." My stomach growled. "But my stomach has other ideas. You shouldn't have mentioned the 'b' word."

He laughed. "You mean breakfast?"

My stomach grumbled again. "That would be the one." I laughed. "Argh. I want to stay here with you."

"Me too, but the world awaits. Come on." He reclaimed his arms, sat up, and scrubbed his hands over his face.

We dressed and headed downstairs. Ma'am sat at the kitchen table with toast and a cup of tea in front of her. In the middle of the table was a plate full of pancakes. Small dishes containing cream, jam, and butter sat next to it, as did a bottle of maple syrup. If I didn't know better, I'd think she was trying to cheer me up. I smiled.

It worked.

I went to the coffee machine and turned it on. "Thanks, Angelica. You didn't have to make breakfast."

Will sat at the table. "But we're glad you did." He started filling his plate with food.

I grabbed the coffee grounds out of the fridge and loaded up the machine.

"What are you doing, dear?"

I turned around and looked at her. "Making coffee."

She waved a hand dismissively. "I can see that. Don't be daft. Why aren't you using your magic?"

I put a cup under the coffee spout and pressed the magic button that would make it all happen—okay, so it wasn't actually magic, but it produced a magical dark liquid. "What if they can find something out about my magic if I use it? Or what if they can feel when I'm using it and control me, make me do something I don't want to do? Or what if they can tell how strong my magic is, or even what I can do with it. The less they know, the better." While the coffee dribbled into my cup, I frothed my milk. No one could talk over the noise, thank goodness. Maybe I didn't feel like pancakes after all. My stomach gurgled. "Stop making me feel guilty," I said. "It's not all about you, you know." I stopped frothing and poured everything into the same cup, then sprinkled chocolate powder over the top and sat next to Will.

"Who were you talking to, dear?"

"My stomach."

Ma'am shook her head. "Just eat, please. You're going to need your strength." That didn't sound good.

"What for?"

"More tests this afternoon. Beren and Dr Finnegan are working on some counter spells. They're going to have to cast them on you later. The faster we unravel that thing, the better. And, by the way, there is no way they can control you. They would need a circle of thirteen to even attempt to create the power they'd need to do that from a distance, and no one has been able to successfully make a circle for hundreds of years."

I grabbed a pancake and smeared strawberry jam and cream on it. "Why not?"

"You need a conduit, a tornado—an extremely powerful witch who is also born with the talent to syphon other people's power. No one like that exists, as far as I know. There may be a few witches with the talent to take small amounts of another witch's freely given energy, but unless they've specifically tried to channel magic from the source river through twelve other witches simultaneously, they'd never know. The magic needed would be extraordinary and likely to kill them and possibly the witches they're working through. Like I said, the witch with that much strength is rarer than hen's teeth."

"Okay. Thanks. I feel a bit better. But what about reading my talents?"

Will swallowed a mouthful of food. "That's pretty unlikely too. Your talent is something that speaks to the source directly, and there won't be a telltale symbol left behind when you practice it. You ask your magic for what you want, yes?" I nodded. "Right, but you don't concoct a spell to go with it. You never have, have you?"

I shook my head. "Oh, wow, okay. And I can think my spell rather than say it out loud in that case, can't I?"

Will nodded, and Ma'am's mouth curved ever so slightly upwards, appreciation shining from her eyes. I would have taken a photo if I'd had time to take the phone out of my pocket and block my magic before her poker face returned. Those moments of praise, even if solely a facial expression, were also rarer than hen's teeth.

"So, can we talk about the case. Or am I a listening-in risk?"

Ma'am sipped her tea, then placed the cup back on the saucer. "We're 99 percent sure they can't hear anything, but we need to confirm it, which will hopefully happen later today. Beren and the doctor are trialling spells now. That is the easiest one to figure out, so they're starting there."

"In that case, can you give me some rough ideas on what's happening? And has anyone else taken the leap?" Not that the stupid snake group would be interested in what crimes we were solving, but you never knew if they were involved.

Ma'am nodded. "Yes, I can. Our agents intercepted one of the victims last night and brought her to the PIB. We've confirmed that after interference, her desire to carry out her objective disappeared. We also spoke to her about what she'd bought and checked it out to find that it is, indeed, faulty. We've decided to stake out the place she received the product, but we need someone who is particularly sensitive to other people's magic use so we can prove later who cast the spell. Once we do this, we will have jurisdiction to execute our search warrant." She picked up her tea and sipped, all the while staring at me meaningfully.

I nodded. "Right." Once I was there, the RP would know where the whole thing was and would likely be watching me, but then again, maybe they couldn't hear us and would have no idea it was a PIB thing, considering the agents would be hiding around the place. Plus, I'd ultimately have the agents' protection. Something that made me feel slightly better, too, was that if killing me was what RP wanted, that guy would have tried instead of just slapping a tattoo on me. But what of those rogues mentioned in the letter? Did they really exist, or was that meant to scare me? I sighed. Whatever it was, I was going to help the PIB. Saving lives was important, and so many more people would be maimed and possibly die if we didn't shut this thing down now. "When is all this happening?" I asked casually before drinking some coffee.

Angelica's magic tingled my scalp as she wrote in the air with her finger. Bright-blue writing shimmered above the table, following her pointer finger. *In one hour. Agent Blakesley will take you. Now, no more questions.*

I nodded. "Is anyone going to have that last pancake?"

"No, dear, it's all yours."

I looked at Will for confirmation. He patted his stomach. "Five's enough for me."

Five! Sheesh, this was only my second. I was letting my stomach down. Will's stomach must have felt much more appreciated. "Thanks." I stabbed the pancake and tried not to think about what was coming.

※

Dr Ezekal's surgery was tucked away in a laneway off the main street that ran through Westerham. There was a fenced car-parking area that led to the single-level 1970s red-brick building. Apparently, he did minor cosmetic surgeries here and the more complicated ones in the hospital. Today he was here. Will had parked opposite the parking-area entrance. Beren sat in the front passenger seat, and Imani and I sat in the back of the Range Rover, which was under a no-notice spell. A car containing another four agents sat behind us, awaiting our signal. They didn't know, of course, that I was the one giving the signal to storm the place—they figured Will was monitoring the situation. The less everyone knew about my special talents, the better.

We'd been here for twenty minutes, and one patient had exited the building, and two had gone in. So far, no magic had disturbed my scalp, but I was focussed, waiting. As soon as I sensed it, I was to tell Will. Then all the agents, except one, would rush in. Imani was staying in the car with me. Will was going to apprehend whatever witch was doing this, and the other agents were going to serve the warrant and search the place. Once Will had the witch in custody, we'd drive to the PIB, and I was to confirm the feel of power. How they were going to force a witch to channel magic, I didn't know, but I supposed they had their ways.

The weather was overcast and drizzling. An old lady with a pink umbrella walked past the car, followed by a younger man with no umbrella, his shoulders hunched and head down against the light rain, both on their way to the main street. There were a couple of other commercial buildings back here, but if anyone saw the guys running into the surgery, they'd just assume they were plain-clothes police or something.

No one spoke, and even though this seemed like a straightforward operation—at least as far as I could tell—the tension in the car had the air practically vibrating. Will, Beren, and Imani were experienced and took on danger without hesitation, but there were unknowns in this operation. We had no idea who the witch actually was, or how powerful they were. Plus, the patients and workers were all non-witches, so there would be much mindwiping later if anything of a magical nature occurred. The rest, they could explain away as being government operatives. And no one wanted an innocent to get hurt if there was crossfire.

Lightning flashed. One one thousand, two one thousand three one thou— *Boom*! I clapped my hands over my ears, and Imani and I looked at each other, eyes wide. Talk about loud thunder.

And then came a pulsing, sibilant cacophony. Torrential rain. The kind of weather you had to yell over to be heard.

But magic didn't have to yell. I sensed it loud and clear.

Magic coming from the surgery caressed my scalp before increasing in pressure. It was almost as if it were trying to force its way under my skin. But it didn't hurt. It was more the insistence of it. Every now and then, its intensity waned before spiking again. The magic held within it contradictions—unsure then determined, ashamed then proud. I'd never experienced anything like it. There was almost a stop-start quality to it—the flow was... off.

I waited another minute, let it sink into my memory—I

needed to be sure later, and I wanted to make certain I felt everything there was to feel about it.

Looking in the rear-view mirror, I met Will's gaze and nodded. That was the cue. His eyes said thank you. He turned to Beren. "Let's go." They jumped out of the car and ran, the agents in the car behind following. The thuds of the doors on the car locking simultaneously were barely audible above the rain.

I hoped I hadn't made a mistake. The magic had seemed like it was coming from the surgery, but we were further away than I would've liked to magic ground zero. What if it had been coming from the building behind or next door? I would be in a whole lot of trouble. But what I did wasn't easy. Surely they'd forgive me. My chest tightened, and I slunk back into my seat, nervousness bringing my finger to my mouth so I could chew a nail. The guys disappeared into the building.

Imani leant over and slapped my hand away from my mouth. "Nasty habit, love."

I pursed my lips and narrowed my eyes at her. "It's all I have."

She rolled her eyes. "You can be such a drama queen. Everything's going to be fine. You'll see."

I stared at her, brought my finger to my mouth, and chewed on another nail. I raised a brow, daring her to slap me again. She smiled and shook her head. "You're a right nutte—"

Her door handle rattled. A man walking past the car had stopped and was trying to open her door. What the hell?

When it didn't open, magic tingled my scalp. Crap. The locks unclicked. He tried to pull the door open, but Imani held it shut. I accessed my power and assessed that she had her return to sender up, but so did he. I hurriedly put mine up as my door opened, and someone grabbed my arm.

I turned.

It was the Greek-looking guy who'd helped poison the tea a few months ago—possibly Dana's boyfriend. His dark eyes crinkled at the corners as he smiled like a shark, and his return-to-sender spell glowed brightly. His magic was strong. So was he. He jerked my arm and ripped me out of the car.

I couldn't let him take me anywhere. Once I was out of sight of my friends, that was it; I'd surely be done for. I faced him, grabbed his shoulder with my free hand, slid my foot behind me, then pulled on his jacket as I thrust my knee up as hard as I could into his groin. He grunted and folded at the waist, but not nearly as much as I'd wanted. His face contorted in pain, but he still managed to glare at me. I tried to push him off, but he wouldn't release my arm.

"Lily!" Imani shouted from behind me.

Dana's friend manoeuvred me around, likely trying to stop Imani from getting behind him. The other RP guy appeared at the front of the car, warily approaching us.

A woman hurried past, head down, pointedly ignoring the situation. I would have screamed for help, but these men were witches and, knowing who they worked for, probably had no compunction about hurting an innocent non-witch—actually, they'd probably relish the opportunity. Bastards.

My heart raced, and the rain saturated me, making my clothes heavy. I tried to yank my arm out of his grasp. He tightened his hand, sending pain up my arm. His friend lunged for Imani, who stepped away, her hands raised in some kind of fighting stance. I was pretty sure she could look after herself, and if I was in danger, her attention would be divided. I needed to figure out how to end this.

One of the moves Will had taught me all those months ago came back. I stepped to the side and made a large circle with my arm, breaking his grip. Surprise registered on his face. At this stage, we needed help. I pivoted and sprinted towards the surgery, ignoring the voice in my head screaming not to leave Imani there. But she was an agent. I had to trust her skills.

Loud breaths came from behind me, and then a body rammed into the back of my thighs, smashing me to the concrete. I landed, arms sprawled in front. My chest and stomach took most of the sharp impact. All the air left my lungs in an "Oomph!" Evil Snake Man had tackled me.

The stinging in my palms barely registered as I tried to jerk my legs from his hold. One of his arms released me, but the other held tight. I looked back. Oh, crap.

He'd pulled a gun.

"Come quietly, or I'll kill you." His deep voice held the hint of a Greek accent, like he'd moved here as an older child. I lashed out with my foot and tried to kick the hand with the gun. He laughed, then stopped abruptly, anger burning from his eyes. "There's no time for this." He looked up and past me to the surgery, from which three different magics pinged my senses.

In my peripheral vision, Imani wrestled on the ground with the other guy. They rolled into a puddle as she tried to get a chokehold on him.

I tried to pull my leg free, and the Greek guy aimed his gun at my leg. "Don't think I won't."

I froze. Tears wanted to come, but I held them back. This was crazy. Helplessness tried to drown me as sure as the downpour did. But I wasn't going to let him take me somewhere.

Our gazes met as I opened myself to the flow of magic.

"You know if you throw a spell at me, it will bounce back to you? I promised to take you back alive, so whatever it is, make sure it isn't deadly." He smirked.

I swallowed. The gun was so black, so pointing at me. "I know what a return to sender is. I'm not stupid. Unlike you. Moron." Maybe if I goaded him enough, he'd do something stupid without thinking, something that gave me an advantage.

His eyeballs almost popped out of their sockets as he puffed up with rage. He pointed at my leg and pulled the trigger. I screamed as the bullet burned through my leg. Seemed as if I'd made a huge error in judgement. The man laughed. "And you thought I wouldn't do it. Yes, I promised to take you back alive, but sometimes I break my promises."

A wave of nausea rippled through me as I gripped my calf muscle, blood seeping through my fingers, reddening the puddle beneath. Gritting my teeth and doing my best to ignore the pain, I drew on my power. I wove a spell in my mind and told it not to activate until I said the word. "You'll never break another promise again, lacky boy. You just shot the wrong witch."

He raised his gun, pointing it at my face.

"Now," I whispered to the swirling magic in my belly.

My doorway formed, the base of it slicing into his upper back—an invisible guillotine—severing it from the lower half. Gruesome, I know, but I didn't want to take any chances. I told myself it was all fake, like a TV show. *It's not real, Lily. It's not real.*

He was dead before he could scream.

Horrified at what I'd done and unable to rise because of the all-encompassing pain, I couldn't physically help Imani, but she looked as if she had things under control. Her hair in ringlets plastered to her face, she knelt behind the guy, who was also on his knees. Her arm circled his neck as she applied the choke. His hands gripping her arm slid off and fell limply at his sides. Then his eyes closed. Imani released him, letting him drop forward, his face smashing on the ground. She pulled magical handcuffs from her inside jacket pocket and cuffed him.

Although, if he was working for RP, he'd likely be dead soon. None of them survived for questioning. We weren't sure, but we thought they were under some kind of spell that prevented them from ever giving out information on the group. If not that, it was poison each one had taken before we could question them. In any case, it was unlikely this guy would be alive in twenty-four hours.

Once Imani locked the guy in the car, she ran to me. "Are you okay, love? Let me see that." She gave no heed to the two pieces of bad guy on the ground. If she wasn't going to mention it, neither was I. As she spelled my leg to stop the bleeding and pain, I slapped a no-notice spell on the Greek guy. There was no point scaring passers-by. At least there hadn't been any for a while because of the sheeting rain.

"Can you stand? It might hurt, but I've contained the bleeding and hopefully most of the pain."

"I'll try. I don't want to lie in this puddle all day." I attempted a smile, but my lips didn't want to cooperate.

Imani helped disentangle me from the dead man and stand. As soon as I was safely balanced on both legs, she looked down at him. "Wow, I've never seen a doorway used like that before. Effective. You can close it now."

I cancelled the doorway—they normally disappeared a few seconds after you'd stepped out, but since it had gone *through* someone rather than the other way around, it hadn't disappeared. "Hmm, yes, very effective. I didn't want to kill him, but he had his return to sender up, and he was pointing a gun at my face. I only had one chance to save myself."

"I know, and I think you did a good job. We do what we must, love. We do what we must." She glanced around, maybe making sure we were safe. "The magic's stopped in there. Why don't we get you to the infirmary and that other thug into a cell; then I'll contact Will and tell him what's happening."

"Sounds good to me."

Imani magicked a camera to herself, took numerous shots of the deceased and the scene for evidence and the incident report. Then, casting a spell that took an enormous gush of energy, she created a dome over the dead man, making him invisible to non-witches. Once that was done, she safely sent his body to the PIB morgue—there was no one watching from the street, but who knew what little eyes watched from the various windows overlooking the laneway.

Imani pulled out her phone, pressed the screen a few times, and held it to her ear. "You guys done?" she asked, then waited. "Aha. Okay. Send B out, and we'll take him back with us. We have a prisoner." Will's raised voice screeched out of the phone, and Imani held it away from her ear. When he'd finished, she put it back and said, "We're all okay. I'll fill you in later, but right now, I want to get Lily to the infirmary. She's fine, but she needs her leg checked out. I'll explain later. Okay, bye."

"I guess we can't just *travel* out of here?"

"No, and I don't have enough power to make another dome to hide everything. We've caused enough of a ruckus out here for one day. You never know who's watching." She looked around, then back at me. Lightning flashed, but this time the thunder took longer to crash, and it wasn't as loud.

Beren came jogging out of the surgery, and Imani and I hopped in the car—her in the driver's seat, me next to her. Beren could watch our criminal in the back. As she drove us back to the PIB, we all dripped mercilessly on Will's leather seats—I hoped he had leather protection on them, or we were all going to be in trouble, but then again, he could probably fix it with magic. Most things could be dealt with that way. Unfortunately there was one thing that couldn't be. Dana's anger.

I'd just killed someone she likely cared about.

I hadn't just poked the piranha, I'd stabbed it with a massive stick, and I wasn't looking forward to her reaction. A stone of dread broke the surface of my contemplation and sunk to the bottom, a weight to remind me of what was yet to come.

And I'd bet my Nikon none of it was good.

CHAPTER 19

Back at the PIB, Dr Finnegan spelled me to sleep, took out the bullet, and healed me. It all took about fifteen minutes, but exhaustion lingered. Now I stood in a room that looked into an interview room via a two-way mirror. It was just like being in a TV show. Imani, Liv, and I listened to the interview Will and Ma'am conducted with Dr Ezekal's daughter as they sat opposite her across a rectangular table. I had no idea why they were interviewing her—her aura clearly showed she was a non-witch.

Imani and I shared a glance, and she shrugged. Well, if she didn't know what was going on, I'd have to stay clueless until Ma'am and Will had finished with her.

"We'll be recording this interview. Please state your name and date of birth for the record," Will said.

"Miranda Anna Ezekal. I'm… I'm not sure of my birth

date. I've always used the 24th of March, 1981, but my parents admitted that it was just an assumption." Her meek voice was quickly swallowed by the sparsely furnished room, and I only just made out what she'd said.

Ma'am leaned forward, clasping her hands and resting them on the desk. "We've done our usual searches, and we couldn't find your birth certificate. Any idea why?"

"I was adopted when I was about one-month old." Still, shouldn't she have a birth certificate?

"Okay, we'll come back to that," said Ma'am. "You've waived your right to a solicitor. Is that correct?"

"Yes." She took a deep breath, then sighed, her shoulders drooping and her head hanging down.

"You do realise these are serious charges—mind control and murder? You're looking at life in prison if you're convicted."

She looked up at Ma'am and nodded, tears falling down her face, mascara smudged and darkening the bags under her eyes. "I'm tired. I can't keep doing this. I didn't want to do it in the first place, but… there was no other way." What was she talking about? Had she paid someone to cast the spells? How could Ma'am be trying to pin this on her?

"Can you show me what you did, Miranda?" The woman widened her eyes, likely shocked at being asked to do what she was about to be tried for. "It's okay. You can just start to do the spell. Why don't you perform half of it, then let it unravel?"

She nodded and closed her eyes. When she opened them and took Will's hand, familiar magic cascaded down my scalp. It was her! I employed my other sight to view her aura. And there it was—the colour indicating she was something other than a non-witch. Normally witches had a solid colour. Hers was blue with clear patches. Spots opened and closed in her aura, the colour filling the holes that appeared before emptying again. Filling, emptying, filling, emptying.

Ma'am held up her hand. "You may stop now."

Once she stopped, the aura faded, and she looked like a plain non-witch. Imani's eyes were wide, but Liv had no idea what was going on because she couldn't feel or see anything. She looked at me with a questioning expression. I mouthed, "Later." She nodded.

Ma'am stood. "Just a moment." That was my cue to quietly meet her in the hallway. I was out there by the time she exited and shut the door behind her. She whispered, "Was that it?"

I nodded. "Definitely. But what's going on? Is she hiding her aura? I didn't even know it was possible, unless you have all your magic blocked, which she didn't."

"No. She's a wilder. They're extremely rare. They only happen when one parent is a witch and one a non-witch, and not in all cases, of course, or you and James would be wilders. We can't find any evidence of her birth records, so she was likely given away by someone who didn't go through the normal channels. Her adoptive parents probably have no idea she's a witch, or even that witches exist. But we have more questions to ask. I'm sure you'll know everything once this interview is done. Now I have to get back to it." I hurried back to my room, and she returned to hers.

All I could think as I watched through the glass was, why? She didn't seem like a bad person. Why kill all those people? Unwanted sympathy momentarily softened my hatred of what she'd done. Because her parents weren't witches, turning twenty-four must have been a scary time. If Angelica hadn't swooped in and educated me that day, I didn't know what I would have done. Probably burn out a hundred coffee machines and give up photography or feel like I was going mad with all the see-through people in my pictures. Although, if James hadn't been kidnapped, surely he would have returned home and explained.

Ma'am resumed the questioning. "So, why have you been spelling people and making them kill themselves?"

She scrunched her eyes tight, then opened them but gazed at the table, unwilling or unable to meet Ma'am's stare. "No one made me do it. It was all my idea."

"That's not what I asked."

"My father. He's getting old… too old to be operating, but other than me, it's all he has. After Mum died ten years ago, he's been obsessed with work. It's the only thing that makes him happy. They adopted me when Mum couldn't have children." She rubbed her nose. "They saved me. I know they did." She finally looked up at Ma'am. "And I wanted to make him happy. Without his work, he'd die. I know he would."

"Okay, go on."

"His skill has gone downhill, and he was making so many mistakes. I started off just wanting to make the flaws invisible to the patients and the people around them, make them happy with the way they looked. If my dad got sued and lost his licence, he'd never forgive himself. I didn't want him to see what he'd really done. I think his eyesight isn't all that good, and he thinks he's doing a good job. Anyway, the spells took too much energy to maintain, and after three or four patients, I realised I couldn't do this with hundreds of people, if it came to that. So when they're in recovery, and I'm monitoring them, I spell them so there's a glamour covering the faults, and I program in a desire to kill themselves in a few months to a year. I didn't want them dying too soon after surgery, or my dad would get blamed for that too, but I guess I failed anyway." She blinked back tears and covered her face with her hands.

But wasn't she sorry she killed people? All her grief appeared to be for her father and what he would lose. What about all those innocents who died?

"And your father never asked you to do this?"

She dropped her hands into her lap, her eyes full of self-loathing and anger when she looked up at Ma'am. "Of course not! He's a kind man. He and Mum took me in when no one would. And he doesn't know what I am. What an evil person I am. Am I possessed?"

Ma'am's poker face dropped for a second—which was enough for me to see the anguish on her face. She shook her head slowly. "No, Miranda. You're not possessed. Although some people may say we are. You're a witch, just like me, like Agent Blakesley here. I'm afraid that after your trial, you'll have a long time to learn about who and what you are while you're in jail with others of our kind. I have one other question." Ma'am took her shrug as acquiescence. "You refused to let in other witches. How did you know they would see through the spell?"

She shook her head. "I didn't know what they were, just that they were like me. They have fuzzy light around them that other people like my mum and dad don't have. We hardly ever get them coming in, but I figured it would be a bad idea, just in case they could tell what I was doing. And if I was evil, surely they were too. I didn't want to think what they might do to me if I tried to make them kill themselves, and I couldn't do anything that left my dad's mistakes exposed."

"Okay. We'll have more specific questions for you later. For now, Agent Blakesley will escort you to your holding cell."

I hated that I felt sorry for her. Maybe if someone had been there for her, she would know she wasn't evil, although killing all those people made her assumptions true. We waited until Will had taken her away, then we all filed into the hallway. Ma'am pinned Imani and I with her unwavering stare. "You two, in my office. Now."

Damn. Just when I thought I was home free. You'd think I'd know better by now. Maybe I was more sloth than squirrel when it came to learning my lessons. Ma'am led the way with an impatient, no-nonsense gait.

Seated in her office, the door closed, she stared with Imani. "I've received your all-too-brief report on the laneway incident. Is there anything you'd like to add?"

Imani's back remained straight, and she didn't even flinch. "No, Ma'am."

Ma'am's gaze floated across the space between Imani and I until it landed on me. "I'd like to hear what happened from your point of view, dear." Why did she say it like it was all my fault? I was an innocent recipient of unwanted kidnap and murder attempts. She looked at her watch, then back at me. "Now would be a good time. I don't have all night."

Argh! "Um... well... Imani and I were waiting for the agents to do their thing in the surgery, and the man who's now in the cells tried to open Imani's door. While that was happening, Piranha's friend opened my door and dragged me outside. We fought for a while, and he said he was going to take me somewhere. When I wouldn't give in easily, he shot my leg. Then he threatened to kill me, so I killed him first. He had a gun pointed at my face and a return to sender up. What else was I supposed to do?"

"You felt you had no other recourse?"

I shook my head emphatically. "No! He even said he was going to kill me. He'd already shot me, for goodness' sake. I believed him. Not to mention the pain and shock I was in. Getting shot isn't exactly on my list of things to do when I'm trying to think through a difficult situation. I'm more aware than anyone of my growing body count." If there were such things as heaven and hell, I was definitely going to be pressing B100 in that lift. I slammed my back against the chair and folded my arms.

"That's all well and good, and I'm not bothered that you killed him, but there's something you need to know." Why did she sound like *need* to know wasn't *want* to know? She held her hand up. A photo appeared in it. She leaned across the table and gave it to me. "This photo was featured on Dana's Instagram account two weeks ago. There are no distinguishing landmarks, so it gives us no indication as to where they were, but if you thought she hated you before, I'm afraid you're going to have to multiply that by about a thousand."

I stared at the picture, as did Imani. She gasped. I could hardly breathe. My stomach dropped as if I were on a rollercoaster.

I'd killed Dana's new husband.

I didn't want to be scared, but I was. And who could blame me?

I couldn't have picked a bigger stick to poke her with if I'd tried.

※

That night, Angelica, Will, and I sat around the dining-room table—Liv was still staying at Beren's until we figured more of this tattoo thing out. We'd just finished dinner, and Will's phone rang. "Hey, B. Yes? Okay, that's great. Yep, first thing tomorrow. I'll let her know. Mmhmm. Will do. Bye." Will smiled at me. "Beren said they've worked out the tracking part of the spell, and they want you there first thing in the morning so they can unravel it. They're also more confident that they can work out the confusion spell, but they still think it's going to take a few weeks."

After the day I'd had, I'd take that as a win. "Yay." Will gave me a thumbs down. Okay, so my yay was a bit pathetic, but I really was happy that I wasn't going to be tracked like a parcel anymore. "I mean it. I'm just tired."

He put his arm around me and kissed the top of my head. "I'm just glad you're alive. Nice work on chopping him in half."

Ma'am smiled. "Yes, dear, it was rather quick thinking. I bet he didn't know if he was coming or going." She laughed. My mouth dropped open in horror. She really did have the most morbid sense of humour ever.

Pride shone from Ma'am's eyes. "And look what we've achieved. The PIB team did it again. There will be fewer suicides at Dover, and all the other patients who are now realising they've had shoddy plastic surgery can sue the doctor and hopefully get on with their lives. And as something extra, I've donated money to a counselling service, to help people with non-witch-induced depression. There are far too many suicides nowadays, and this case has been a terrible reminder of that. Anyway, you should all be proud of yourselves. Thank you for helping out today, Lily. I'm sorry it put you in harm's way."

"It's not your fault." I shrugged. The only one to blame was Dana and whoever ran the snake group. "We'll get to the bottom of it eventually, and then we won't have to worry." And that day couldn't come too soon.

"Too true." Ma'am stood. "Time to clear the table." She

waved her arm, and everything disappeared. Well, that was one way—okay, the best way—to do it.

My phone rang. "Hey, James. Is everything all right?"

"Yes, although shouldn't I be asking you that question? Maybe you need two bodyguards. If I lost you…" He cleared his throat. "Anyway, how's your leg?"

I swallowed my emotion and flexed my calf muscle. "Hmm, seems good as new. I'm a bit freaked out by the whole thing, and my ears are still ringing, but I should be fine. How's the baby?" Changing the subject to something happier seemed the best thing to do.

"Well, that's the other reason I was calling." Happiness blossomed in his voice.

"Ooh, yes? Do tell."

"She finally has a name. Annabelle Lily Katarina Bianchi."

This time I let the tears well in my eyes. "Oh my God, you named her after me and Mum? Tell Mill thank you. I love you guys."

"We love you too. If you're feeling up to it, wanna come have lunch with us tomorrow?"

I grinned. "I would love to! Does Mill want me to bring anything?"

"Nope, just yourself. See you around eleven thirty?"

"Done. See you then."

Ma'am smiled down at me. "It's good to see you happy. I know you've been through so much since I dragged you over here, and I know I don't tell you as often as I should, but I'm proud of you."

I blinked back more tears and held onto the table so I didn't fall off my chair. I smiled back. "You don't tell me at all, but thanks." I laughed. "But seriously, thank you. The fact that I have you both, and I can go and visit my brother whenever I want, makes up for everything else. Thanks for being there for me too."

I stood and hugged Angelica. Then Will stood and wrapped his arms around both of us. Joy surged through me, carrying my worries away.

Best ending to the day ever and one I never would have seen coming this morning. Seemed I didn't hate every surprise after all.

ALSO BY DIONNE LISTER

Paranormal Investigation Bureau

Witchnapped in Westerham #1

Witch Swindled in Westerham #2

Witch Undercover in Westerham #3

Witchslapped in Westerham #4

Witch Silenced in Westerham #5

Killer Witch in Westerham #6

Witch Haunted in Westerham #7

Witch Oracle in Westerham #8

Witch Cursed in Westerham #10

The Circle of Talia

(YA Epic Fantasy)

Shadows of the Realm

A Time of Darkness

Realm of Blood and Fire

The Rose of Nerine

(Epic Fantasy)

Tempering the Rose

ABOUT THE AUTHOR

USA Today bestselling author, Dionne Lister is a Sydneysider with a degree in creative writing, two Siamese cats, and is a member of the Science Fiction and Fantasy Writers of America. Daydreaming has always been her passion, so writing was a natural progression from staring out the window in primary school, and being an author was a dream she held since childhood.

Unfortunately, writing was only a hobby while Dionne worked as a property valuer in Sydney, until her mid-thirties when she returned to study and completed her creative writing degree. Since then, she has indulged her passion for writing while raising two children with her husband. Her books have attracted praise from Apple iBooks and have reached #1 on Amazon and iBooks charts worldwide, frequently occupying top 100 lists in fantasy. She's excited to add cozy mystery to the list of genres she writes. Magic and danger are always a heady combination.